A DECISION
WITH
DEVASTATING
CONSEQUENCES

By

A.H. Howard

Thanks a million for going through my manuscript for me. Best regards, Brenda.

To my family with all my love.

CHARACTERS:

Abdulla Hussain   *Main Character*

Siobhan O'Rourke   *Main Character*

Padraig, Siobhan's fiancé   *Main Character*

Liam and Bridget are Siobhan's parents

JP, and Sean are Siobhan's brothers

Jim, a cousin and Marreese his friend

Landlords of the large estate in Co Cork, Albert and Julie, Herbert

Arsalan and Abeer Hussain. Abdulla's parents

Ahmed Hussain is his Brother

Siobhan's children Orla Fatima, and Jonathan Arslan, and Cathal

Siobhan's uncle Tim

Raham, Orla, and Jonathan's friend

Trudy and Amahil, close friend of Siobhan and her brother JP

CHAPTER 1

Abdulla confronts his father

'No, no, no, I am not marrying that girl, the one you call "one of our own kind!" No, I want more out of life. What's wrong with you people?' Abdulla shouted at his father.

The angry young man felt crushed by the pressures of a life he did not want to belong to anymore.

'Are you all stupid? Take a look around you for once in your pathetic little lives,' he roared with contempt.

Life in Lahore, Pakistan, was just not good enough for him anymore – there was so much more of the world to see. He was finally ready to leave for the new country he longed to be a part of – he wanted to be thought of as a 'British citizen'. It sounded so good to him. He had heard so much about Great Britain and knew that was where he wanted to be.

'No Father, you won't stop me. Not now!'

'You listen to me now, boy,' said his father, Arslan, as he pinned his son up against the wall and slapped him hard on the shoulder, warning him to show some respect for him and for his country. 'Yes, *your* country!' shouted his father. 'The country of your birth – the country that you, my son, can never get away from. You can't wash it away, because the minute you stand in front of the mirror, who you really are will be staring right back at you.'

Arslan had given in to his son's demands and allowed him to work in the local hotel. And now look how he paid back his father!

'You, my son, are getting above your station! You left a good job working with me, and now you stab your father in the back – you're an ungrateful scoundrel!'

'Well, I want out,' said Abdulla, holding back with all his might the urge to strike his father. He would not do as he was told, or be ordered around anymore. Now was his time to break for freedom and not to be tied to his father or this family any longer. At last, he was about to become a free man.

'Son, do you understand me?' said his father, in a desperate effort to reassert his power as head of the family. Abdulla *would* marry this girl and there was no more to be said on the matter according to his father.

Yes, there was no more to be said, thought Abdulla. His father had ruled his family with fierce brutality all his life. Arslan glared over his shoulder at his son and stormed out of the room, slamming the heavy door behind him. As far as Arslan was concerned, his word was set in stone.

Ahmed, Abdulla's younger brother, was very fearful of his father. Each evening, when Arslan dominated the family over dinner, merely sitting down beside his father made Ahmed feel sick as Arslan spat his half-eaten food all over the table. He never talked like a normal person. He just bawled at everyone around him, including Ahmed's mother Abeer.

From the age of four, Ahmed had developed a severe stammer, much to his father's contempt.

'You fix him, do you hear me?' Arslan raged at his wife. 'Fix him and don't let him make a show of his family or there will be consequences for bearing such a stupid delicate boy. Why didn't you give me a second strong son?' He slapped his wife across the face in an act of complete brutality.

'Why? You've made me the laughingstock of the town, having a stupid halfwit son. "Look at poor Arslan, with a halfwit of a boy" –

that's what everyone is saying about me,' he roared, as he vented his anger on his terrified wife.

Many times, Ahmed thought of running away from his father, but where would he go? And who would put up with the likes of him? If he left, would his life be in more danger? Was a life like his worth living at all, he wondered.

He had decided many years ago that he would never give his father anything to complain about. He would comply with Arslan's unreasonable wishes, whatever he demanded. He worked even harder at making mudbricks with him. He tried to earn his respect, even to the detriment of his health.

The more Ahmed tried to answer his father when he asked a question, the angrier his father became. He was always so angry and Ahmed just couldn't get the words out of his mouth. The more he tried the worse he got … until he could not speak at all.

His father threatened him with the asylum, telling him that he would send him there. He was no son of his, he told him. He was only a halfwit.

The boy wondered if the asylum would be a mercy for him, a way of getting away from this brutal monster. Maybe he would have a life better than the one he was living at home?

Abdulla was relieved that he had some savings of his own and all the paperwork ready for his break away from his family, from all that he detested about his country. It was a move that would transform his world and his life completely. After all, he was 22 years old and ready.

He was old enough to make his way in the world. London was so popular – people from all over the world made a new life there. It was the land of great opportunity, if you were prepared to work – whether it was as a chef in one of the top hotels in the city, or in medicine or another professional capacity. The list went on and there was the lifestyle that went with such opportunities. He vowed he would reach great heights there. Finally, he would get away from the traditional shalwar clothing which his father insisted on his sons wearing. He would get to wear smart suits and trendy clothes. He rushed into his bedroom, his blood still boiling and packed his suitcase for the last time in a home and family he would no longer be a part of.

Abdulla never thought of his younger brother when he was making his plans, as he also taunted and ridiculed Ahmed for making a show of him in front of his friends. He knew how much his father detested Ahmed, and the fate he would surely encounter if his father heard enough of his stammering, while he – the golden-haired boy – would be far away living his new life, oblivious to his father's distress at losing his 'trophy' son.

CHAPTER 2

J.P. and Siobhán decide to leave Galway

It was summer 1976. There was no place like Galway at that time of year: the smell of the salty sea air, the heady perfume of wild roses in bloom, the buzz of happy holidaymakers from all over the place and the aroma of local cuisine flowing from busy restaurants as visitors passed by. There was plenty of banter between the locals and tourists that year and music played on every corner.

After much deliberation on whether to stay or go, J.P. O'Rourke and his sister Siobhán had made up their minds. It was as good a time as any. They had decided to start new lives in England where they would be able to make more money – a lot more. London would be their opportunity to start anew and lead more interesting lives.

They had even arranged that they would be met on arrival by their cousin Jim Kendrick, who would help them to settle in.

'There are much better job opportunities for us in London,' J.P. told their parents. 'So what do you think, Dad and Mum?' he asked, looking directly at his father Liam. His mind was already made up – he was asking for the views of his worried parents out of courtesy.

'The pair of ye are old enough,' his father replied, pointing at his eldest child. 'J.P., you're 24 now and you've got your chef's apprenticeship finally finished at the Salthill Hotel, one of the best hotels in Galway.'

'Yes, Dad,' said J.P., who felt he was well qualified to get a good job now.

Liam looked at his daughter. 'And Siobhán, sure what age would you be now? 21? With your training completed as a cook at Madigan's Hotel – sure there's no holding the pair of ye back at all.'

Siobhán could feel her skin prickle all over and that only happened when she was nervous, but she wasn't sure if it was nerves about making such a big move to London, or worry that her parents would only allow J.P. to go. Would they try to hold her back after thinking it through? Deep down she knew her parents could not prevent her from going, but she desperately wanted and needed their blessing.

'Now's the time to make something of yourselves, to see a different side of life,' said their father. Siobhán could not contain the excitement she felt as she threw her arms around her father and hugged him tightly, and then gently kissed her mother. She promised both of them that she would mind herself – and look after her brother. She knew her mother would be delighted that her son was being cared for. Siobhán was the one who polished all the shoes on a Saturday night while J.P. got away with murder! She never held it against him as an adult, but as children they had many a fight over him not doing his fair share of work in the house.

She knew she would miss her ex-boyfriend Pádraig, but sadly there was no commitment from him. She knew she must put him out of her mind and feel as free as a bird. But she also knew that she would miss being near her close friend Marie in Galway. They had grown up together and were very close, but she felt Marie would be alright with Finbar, her long-time boyfriend, so she immediately felt better.

'Well? Isn't it a good idea, Bridget?' said Liam as he looked in the direction of his wife, who was wiping her wet hands on her well-worn bib. He waited for some words of reassurance from her.

'At least it's not Australia – there's a small mercy in that,' said Bridget. (She worried about those big planes they would travel in on their way to London. They would have no chance if anything happened so high up in the sky.) Bridget thought back to when her children had relied on her for everything and felt an ache in her heart. At that very moment she just wanted to throw her arms around the two of them and mind them forever, never letting her babies go. 'You'll only be across the pond now,' she said gently. With that lightness in her voice, she tried to hide how she really felt about their departure.

'And if you decide to come back in a while, there would be no shame in that – at least you would have tried,' said their mother. But she knew once they had flown the nest, it was unlikely they would return home again to live … it would be just the occasional holiday visit. That was what most people did once they left Ireland for work and a better life. It would be the end of the world she had known she thought sadly, while trying to hide her true feelings.

'They will easily pick up a job someplace in London, with all its grand hotels,' she said. She was glad her children were brave enough to make such an important move to a land they had never known, changing their entire lives as they made their way out into the unknown.

The O'Rourke's lived on a small farm on the outskirts of Galway city. The younger son Sean never looked tidy – his long dark hair fell down over his eyes, half blinding him, and he always put up a fight against going to the barbers for a haircut.

'You'll go blind, Sean if you don't get that hair shortened, do ya hear me?' asked Bridget, scolding her youngest son in a kind-hearted way – he was the apple of her eye.

'Ah sure, what's the point, Mam?' He used every excuse in the book to avoid a haircut.

If he was not helping his daddy, he was fixing his bike: taking it apart and then putting it back together again. He was the third and youngest child – nine years old and a late baby, as he was described. Bridget had got 'caught on the change', a talking point whenever someone was curious about the difference in the children's ages.

'He'll be with us for a long while yet,' said Liam to his wife. 'Now that the other two are finally off our hands.' He teased his wife but he still felt a sense of acute loss. 'Well, we won't be lonely anyhow. Plenty of noise with him rattling around with that auld bike of his – nuts and bolts everywhere.'

'But I wouldn't have it any other way,' said Bridget. 'What would we do if we were left with just a tidy house … no laughter or chat from Sean and all the young lads?'

For such a young chap, he seemed a lot older than his years. Maybe it was because he had grown up with much older siblings, thought Bridget.

'All the same, God was good to us Liam, giving us another chance at rearing again!'

Bob Leandra, the head chef in the Salthill Hotel, had encouraged J.P. to make the move to London, where he knew this exceptionally ambitious young man would rise through the ranks. Bob saw huge potential in terms of a bright future. Even though the West of Ireland was a busy enough place in the summer, with American tourists and other nationalities visiting, business was only seasonal. There would be more money to be made and much more experience to be gained abroad. So he encouraged the pair to take a chance before they met up with their life partners at home and became tied down – ending their chance to experience all that life had to offer in a more rewarding place.

Liam glanced at his wife and remembered when he met her for the first time at the local parish dance: a tall slender young woman with a head of blonde curls. God, he thought, that was a long time ago now, but she could still touch his very soul. Yes indeed, she was definitely his soulmate and he knew there was nothing they would not do for one another. But it had put a stop to his dream of travelling to America to make a new life, with all the opportunities it had to offer at the time. Bridget was then caring for her elderly mother and could not leave Galway, let alone Ireland, so that put paid to that. He knew that life was full of dreamers just like himself. Some manage to make it over the fence and follow their dreams, and some hit the fence and never make their dream come true, for one reason or another. They are the ones who just settle and take what they can from life, without really aiming higher. They long for the unreachable, but responsibilities take hold of them, and they are consumed completely by the chaos of their everyday life – a life they have reluctantly chosen. Bridget saw that faraway look in her husband's eyes and, picking up on it instantly, apologised once again for his lost opportunity.

But he lovingly put his arm around Bridget's shoulder, telling her she was the best thing that had ever happened to him. He could travel all over the world and never meet the likes of her.

'Now our children are taking a giant step out into the world and far away from all they know, into a world full of strangers. Isn't it wonderful when the elusive dream is being captured by their hearts?' said Liam. 'Maybe they are the ones who will really make their dreams come true.'

CHAPTER 3

Settling into life in London

Brother and sister arrived at London's Paddington Station, tired after many hours on a train from Holyhead in Wales, where their ship from Dublin had docked. It had been a rough crossing on the Irish Sea.

'Siobhán, let's get a pot of tea and a few slices of toast – that should sort us out,' said J.P. as they reached the station café.

'God, yeah, I can't wait to get going. Are you as tired as I am?' she asked, glancing at her brother who looked as if he had a good night's sleep behind him and was raring to go. 'I'm shattered, but very excited' she said sleepily.

Jim Kendrick, their first cousin, was there to meet them. When J.P. and Siobhán laid eyes on him, they could see that he had left his Galway lifestyle well behind him. He was now truly a cool Londoner with his red corduroy bell-bottoms and tight, well-worn, brown leather jacket, set off with trendy platform boots. The siblings could not get their heads around how Jim was dressed. J.P. looked at his sister and asked her how they were going to fit into this new life. They both knew they had a lot of work ahead of them, trying to embrace the whole new world their cousin Jim had adapted to so quickly.

Jim was well used to the hectic London life by now and loved his job as a shop assistant in a trendy clothes shop on Chelsea's King's Road. And he had no problem charming the girls as they warmed to this good-looking young Irishman.

Jim did not intend to get married any time soon – he was simply not interested. He liked his life as it was and was not going to be tied down by anybody. With his good looks, his wavy black hair and deep-set brown eyes, he was well able to hold his own against all the cool rivals around him, now that he had become part of swinging London.

Jim could see just how young and timid his cousins were. How were they going to handle life in this big city? As they had stepped off the train they had appeared to be in awe of their unfamiliar surroundings, and Jim remembered that feeling as his own memories flooded back. He had nobody to meet him back then – no one to give him some much-needed advice. He was green behind the ears and found himself at the mercy of all kinds of people in the beginning. They seemed to be horrible people – and he appeared as an innocent, foolish young buck from the Aran Islands, back in Ireland. In the past he thought he knew everything there was to know about life, like all young people, but London was in a different universe and he had to learn fast.

J.P. looked over at his cousin and studied his outfit. *He's so London*, he thought. *And me? Yeah, a real jackass, wet behind the ears – japers, what am I like, he thought?* He tried to smooth out his navy cord pants and fix his dated cream shirt and blue tie, but he knew he was no match for his trendy cousin Jim, the London city slicker.

Jim had found his way around London the hard way. After suffering a bad beating and being left for dead late one night near King's Cross train station, he was found by two young policemen and taken to hospital by ambulance. He spent the best part of two weeks there, recovering from that savage assault. After that, he began to understand that being fresh from Ireland marked him out as being different. He tried not to stand out and his dazzling personality helped him to make friends easily, so most people he met were drawn to him and he began to settle in.

He was lucky to meet some decent young men along the way who looked out for him and taught him how to live life safely in London. He learned how to discern who the scoundrels were and who to trust. He knew how to handle the rowdies back home in Ireland in an honest-to-God fist fight if things became tricky, but London was a different situation. Some fellas would knife you for a couple of bob and a cigarette – that was how bad it was in parts of London.

He had met the roughest people he could possibly imagine and that was how he ended up in hospital. He had little money on him at the time he was robbed, so they gave him a couple of extra punches to the head for not having more … or so they told him before they landed the punch that rendered him unconscious.

Jim could see his Irish cousins now had that same wondrous look of pure panic and excitement all at once. They were well out of their comfort zone and had entered a mad world where all kinds of new experiences had to be encountered. But Jim knew they both wanted to be part of it … eager to blend in as soon as possible.

'Hold on a minute now, lads,' Jim said to his cousins. 'We'll get some tea and toast and a couple of eggs in the station café here before we move on. It'll settle your stomachs.'

Siobhán jumped at the chance to settle down for a chat. God, she had never tasted tea like this before!

'Nothing like the first pot of tea after such a long journey. It's even better than the first mug of coffee or tea in the morning, don't you think?' Jim directed his question at the two young greenhorns.

'Yes. And you can't beat toast with butter melting into it, either!' Just for a moment it felt like home to Siobhán.

She tried to take in everything around her but was distracted by a young woman who was passing by their table. She looked unkempt with her straggly black unwashed hair held back off her face by a thin blue hairband. She was probably about the same age as herself, or maybe a little younger. She was pushing an old pushchair with a crying baby. Siobhán managed to get a look at the child who had a red rash all over her tiny face and she could see that the child had been sick over her little primrose dress. Beads of sweat stood out on the child's forehead and she was in a distressed state. The mother was dressed in a worn pale blue cotton dress with black sandals that had seen better days and, on closer observation, Siobhán saw she was chewing gum, with a cigarette hanging from her left hand. The woman and baby made their way out of the café. Siobhán wondered how she could chew gum and smoke at the same time. The mother was oblivious to the child's crying and its needs.

'God, the poor little thing,' thought Siobhán, and wondered what the woman's story was. What would become of her, and where would the child end up? Siobhán felt she was waking up to a world where lost souls did not seem to matter – a world devoid of human kindness.

She handed over a brown parcel of food to Jim. 'It's from Mam – she says you're to have a good feed.' Inside were white and black puddings and packets of cured bacon, along with a mound of sausages.

'Ah, now we're talking my language, lads. God, Aunty Bridget never forgets me at Christmas and Easter, but this is an added bonus!' His eyes sparkled with delight.

All three finally arrived by taxi at the O'Rourke's new address, 18 Holloway Road, Archway, London, N19. Jim had found them a top floor flat. It was in a large Victorian house that had four two-bedroom flats, each with their own sitting room, kitchen and bathroom. The minute they opened the door, they were hit with the spectacle of heavy dark brown paint peeling off the walls. It was in desperate need of some fresh paint and the smell of damp and cigarettes hit their nostrils as they entered the hallway.

The three climbed up the long dark stairs onto a dingy corridor with outdated brown wallpaper, finally reaching their flat. Jim opened the door for the two young siblings, while acknowledging the bad state of the place.

Siobhán remembered her home comforts, and for a moment she became anxious, until a feeling of excitement took hold of her again. She was talking and rolling her sleeves up at the same time.

'This place is going to need one hell of a scrubbing!' she said with enthusiasm.

She peeped into the bathroom, almost afraid that someone might jump out at her. She looked at the holes in the corners of the old wooden floor – it was as if the mice had a right of way, using a well-worn pathway around the house. But this would be the end of their good times she thought; they would stuff newspapers into the holes to keep the rodents out – and if that didn't work, well they would think of something else. She felt they would figure everything out in time.

'Were these old taps ever working do you think, Jim?' asked J.P. Only a dribble of rusty water was coming out and the pipes were making an unmerciful sound, shaking the floor under them at the same time.

The pink striped curtains on Siobhán's bedroom window were in shreds, but she was lucky to have curtains at all. J.P. had none, so the sunlight would be beating in on top of him first thing in the morning. They would have to tack a pillowcase across the skylight for the time being.

'Janey Mac, lads, would you look at the size of the kitchen!' she called out. It was so tiny there was barely enough room to sit down at the small table. They were used to a big old farm kitchen, with a table to match … but this was not Galway.

Siobhán examined the dilapidated cooker. 'Yep, it's seen better days,' she shouted to Jim. 'I hope it's still working. There's a lot of rust on top and inside the oven.'

With a bit of steel wool and elbow grease, she planned to shine it up like new.

'The last lot were lazy buggers to leave the place in such a state,' said Siobhán and J.P. at the same time, as they both laughed with the excitement and challenge of it all. But what did it say about the greedy landlord, not bothering to make the flat a bit more presentable for his new tenants?

'Not everyone is like that last lot,' said Jim, feeling somewhat annoyed.

The bedrooms had two new single beds, with the wrapping still on them, so Siobhán was pleased with that and Jim had bought his cousins a couple of sets of bedclothes and a couple of pillows. He also threw in a few cushions to get them started.

The poor state of the flat did not make the slightest dent in their happiness at having their own home in London. The huge bay window in the large sitting room brightened up the whole place, much to their delight, so things appeared not so bad after all. Straight away Siobhán was planning how she would pull the place together into something more homely.

To start with, she would buy some blue gingham material to make cushions for the sitting room, and new curtains for her bedroom window, and perhaps throw a couple of bedspreads over the old, faded couch and armchairs. They would need a good scrub first though, as their best days were well and truly behind them.

All sorts of emotions surged through Siobhán's head – happy, sad and fearful. Would she get the right job, or any job at all? Would they be able to fix the flat up with so little money available?

Her thoughts moved to Padraig and she wondered if he would realise she had left Galway at all. It was hard to believe just how close they had been as young teenagers in school and how they had spent so much time coming and going between each other's houses. Siobhán had sat her final school exams and then went on to train as a cook. Padraig had left school two years before her at the age of 16 and found work in a local hardware store, as his parents could not afford to keep him in school any longer, being part of a large family. His father worked around Ireland on building sites, and with Padraig bringing home an extra pay packet, life would be a lot better at home.

Siobhán remembered how much Padraig liked engineering, how he had built a miniature house with only pieces of wire, stone and timber, placing a tiny hose with water flowing from it to make the sink and toilet work, while adding electricity to power a small bulb.

'Oh, why did he give up on his dream,' thought Siobhán, 'leading him to a life destined for hardship?'

All of his friends were amazed at how talented he was. She had always liked him much more than any of the other local boys. They drifted apart when she started working in the hotel because her working hours were not the normal nine to five each day. Occasionally, she would meet up with her group of friends and catch up on all the gossip.

One evening as she walked out of the hotel, Padraig was waiting for her on the porch and asked her if she would like him to walk her home – much to her surprise – but her heart beat a little faster and she knew she liked him more than just a little. But that seemed a very long time ago now.

Jim urged the pair to leave their luggage in the bedrooms as he checked to see if everything else was working. J.P. put his things into the box room, leaving the large bedroom for Siobhán.

'J.P., I don't mind taking the smaller room at all. Sure, I'm just happy that we've finally moved out of home. And Mam and Dad were probably delighted to get rid of us,' said a giggling Siobhán.

'Ah now, I wouldn't go that far, Siobhán,' said J.P., smiling at the prospect of what was facing them both in their new lives.

'It's time to go down to the Archway Tavern to get something to eat,' announced Jim. 'Ye must be starving by now lads.'

'Yes, we just had some toast earlier,' said Siobhán, suddenly feeling very hungry.

'That was hours ago,' said Jim, pulling the flat door open. 'Yeah, that was only to keep the pair of you standing. So would you like some corned beef, cabbage and spuds?'

It was music to their ears and for a moment it almost felt like home. Siobhán had been seasick and couldn't eat on the ship, but now that she was back to normal, she felt she could murder a good dinner.

'You'll always get good grub in the pubs over here and they make an extra effort at weekends. And lads, in time you'll get used to the pork pies and other foods they have already prepared for the supermarkets.'

Has Jim forgotten we've got supermarkets back home, wondered Siobhán but she continued to listen to him out of respect.

J.P. pointed out that he and Siobhán would be eating most of their meals in their workplaces and that he didn't see their small kitchen being a problem at all. They would get to taste all kinds of food prepared for the palettes of different nationalities once they got their jobs organised.

Jim recalled when he was a teenager, employed for the summer in one of the hotels in Galway city. A couple of American teenagers were looking for a peanut butter and jelly sandwich. He couldn't imagine eating the likes of that. Surely it would turn your stomach he had thought. It never seemed to turn their stomachs, however.

Ah, those Americans, a different breed altogether it seemed!

Jim made some practical suggestions over dinner about how to go about looking for a good job in the right area and in the right hotels. Siobhán pulled out a notepad to write down the employment agencies' names. She had prepared letters for herself and J.P. to use when seeking employment and had copies of their references in two folders.

After a good night's sleep they were both awake early. The pipes rattled ominously again as they started to get ready, and the taps started spewing out rusty water before eventually running clear and allowing them to wash. After they had eaten some breakfast cereal, the pair were ready to go job hunting.

Siobhán took one last look in the mirror. She was an attractive young woman, tall, with well-kept long blonde hair and deep blue eyes, and she felt suitably smart in a cream suit with matching brown handbag and high-heeled shoes, although she had a pair of flat pomes for walking around London. She didn't feel as much of a greenhorn as she had felt when arriving at Paddington Station only yesterday, but she knew she was far from being a confident woman of the world in this new place.

J.P. also looked smart with his well-cut dark hair, navy suit, crisp white shirt and smart black leather shoes. He was a person who stood out, a person who would definitely not fade into the background. He looked like a smart businessman with his folder tucked neatly under his arm. Yes, he was a man on a mission.

After a couple of hours, the siblings stopped and had a pot of strong tea and a pastry in a café. They sat quietly and swopped ideas about their job opportunities.

'Well, what do you think, Siobhán?' said her brother.

'God, isn't it a lovely sunny day to be looking for work?' she said. 'Doesn't it make it a lot easier?' she continued, and laughed at how excited she felt.

J.P. laughed even louder at his sister's silly statement.

'London has all the colours of the rainbow on every street, with all of its people and its unfamiliar buildings,' said an eager J.P.

After a long, gruelling day, the pair put their heads together, exhausted but happy. Over their pub dinner they examined their options. They were lucky to have a choice of jobs by then. After much debating, they reached a conclusion about which were the best options.

The Hilton Hotel, not too far from Oxford Street, was Siobhán's choice. The manageress, Miss Ruth Donnelly, had interviewed her for the job and offered it to her there and then. She told Siobhán to let her know tomorrow, after sleeping on it. She hoped Siobhán was a good worker and addressed her as 'Miss O'Rourke'. The fact that Ruth and Siobhán were both Irish was an advantage. It was most probably the deciding factor, along with her excellent references. It probably appealed to the manageress to have one of her countrywomen working with her, someone who understood how things were managed in restaurants back home, while adapting to the special demands of business in London.

J.P. landed a good job in the Royal Hotel, working alongside world-renowned chef Jason MacArthur. His glowing references had helped him secure that top job and 'Mr MacArthur' hoped 'Mr O' Rourke', as he formally addressed J.P., would not prove him wrong. It was alien to J.P.'s ears, but at the same time it sounded good to him.

J.P. and Siobhán took the Underground into work every day, settling into their new lives with all the ups and downs that such an adventure entailed. Siobhán still got a pang in her heart when she thought of Padraig, but knew she needed to get on with her life – there was so much to see and do in this new world of hers.

Jim usually met up with the pair a couple of times a week in the Archway Tavern, to make sure everything was alright.

'I have to admit this place is taking a while to get used to,' said J.P. one evening.

'It took me over a year to settle,' said Jim. 'Just when I was making plans to go back home, all of a sudden I no longer wanted to return.'

He had not realised that multicultural London had grown on him. But he now loved the fact that not everyone was white, and some of his closest friends were African and Pakistani.

'They're a good bunch of lads who look out for one another, though we have our differences and the odd argument – but nothing too serious. What about you, Siobhán?' asked Jim, looking directly at her.

'Sure, like himself,' she said, pointing at her brother, 'I'm still trying to get used to things as best I can.' She straightened herself up to listen more attentively.

'But are you settling in well?' asked Jim.

'I won't be going home with my tail between my legs just yet anyway,' she laughed. 'Most of the staff I work with are alright. You know how things are. You have to take the rough with the smooth and try not to rub anyone up the wrong way. Though no matter how hard you try, some people are just plain cantankerous. I've made one good friend – her name is Trudy. She's from Scotland – did you know that some Scottish people still speak Gaelic? Imagine that! Very like us back home, but not the same of course. Other than that, my boss is very fair to everyone. London is lovely in the summer with most people in good form. So I don't feel out of place or nervous anymore,' said Siobhán.

She had taken on London with great optimism and looked forward to a good future there. She might even meet the man of her dreams. Although maybe not just yet, as she still thought of the man she had left back home in Galway.

CHAPTER 4

Abdulla realises his dream

In August 1976, Abdulla Hussain arrived at London's Heathrow Airport from Lahore, Pakistan, with his friend Amahil Zakie. They were both wildly excited to finally realise their dream of leaving their native country and settling in England, the land of opportunity and freedom. Together, they made their way slowly out of the airport into the sweltering summer heat and into a new life. Abdulla, wearing heavy Pakistani clothes, felt the heat immediately. They had heard that London was much cooler than Pakistan, so they had come prepared.

Abdulla was very excited at the thought of enjoying a brand-new life in Europe, and dreamt of buying a new high-fashion wardrobe. All that would come in time, but first they had to find somewhere to stay. They hailed a taxi outside the airport that took them to a letting agent. The hotel where they were due to be employed had forwarded the name and address of this man. They hoped they would make it to the agency and be able to do business before the close of day, as otherwise they would have to stay in a hotel for the night, eating into their very limited resources. Once they had secured a flat they were free to head for the hotel where their jobs were waiting.

They were lucky to secure a flat in Camden Town at very short notice. It was fairly run-down but it was all they could afford until their first pay cheques arrived. They had limited cash so they needed to be careful. In London, they would live a totally different life, far away from their homeland, making a new start full of adventure and promise.

Abdulla's father had not offered his son any money or help whatsoever. Even if he had, Abdulla told himself, he would not have taken it. Even now, having arrived in Great Britain using his own resources, he was still mad with his angry father over how he had treated him.

Abdulla and Amahil had secured jobs as commis chefs in the Royal Hotel, and it was here they met J.P. for the first time, Abdulla giving him a firm handshake and letting J.P. know that he was a willing worker, and ready to learn the ropes.

With his first pay cheque, Abdulla hurried to some of the top men's clothes shops in London, kitting himself out in the latest fashion. He then visited a Vidal Sassoon hairdressing salon and got a full head of highlights, covering his jet-black hair. He wanted to look like all the other fashionable Londoners – a clean slate, a new man, leaving the dust of his Pakistani homeland far behind him.

With his good looks and charm, he told himself he could achieve whatever he set his mind to. He was fiercely determined to work his way up in the world, and to touch the lives of the people who mattered, people who could be of use to him as he became established.

When he was a child in Lahore, all the men in the family prayed at least five times a day, with Friday a full day of prayer. He and his brother often got a clatter across the head for not paying attention at these events. Abdulla had promised himself that once he got out of Pakistan and landed on English soil, he would leave all that behind him, along with his controlling father and his unfortunate younger brother.

His family were relatively poor. His father and brother earned a living making mudbricks and put in long hours each day. Abdulla had worked with his father from the age of 10. But in his heart he knew that he was just biding his time, knowing he could do a lot better, make something of his life. After many arguments with his father, at the age of 16 he was finally allowed to work in a large hotel in the region, where he put in long hours of hard labour in the kitchen. He learned the art of good cooking and got to understand what the customers liked and demanded. A high standard was expected from everyone who worked in that hotel. Part of his training for a better life was observing and learning from the people around him who mattered.

J.P. got to know Abdulla well as he worked alongside him as his commis chef. He told J.P. that he was more than a little homesick, but in fact he was really just seeking pity, hoping that J.P. would look on him as a friend eventually. He and his friend Amahil were occasionally invited to J.P. and Siobhán's flat for tea to help them to get used to life in London and to relieve their loneliness.

J.P. and Siobhán were happy to help out anyone who was not from Britain – people who were foreign to the country, like themselves. Both of them got on well with Abdulla and Amahil, and they enjoyed sitting around the table, sharing stories from home and discussing how they were settling into their new lives. Abdulla took a liking to Siobhán and she liked him as a friend. She still held a place in her heart for Padraig, and hoped that he missed her as much as she missed him.

She planned to make enough money to go home to Galway and open a restaurant with J.P. at some point – that is, if he also decided to return in a few years. If not, she would still go ahead with her plans when she felt the time was right. She hoped Padraig would still be single, and if not – well, that was a chance she had to take. She didn't mind working hard and saving, and she was more than happy to work any extra hours she was offered.

She lived thriftily, saving as much as she could, buying most of her clothes in markets on Camden Street at the weekends and in vintage shops. Of course, her brother loved to tease her about how frugal she was, but he could hardly tell the difference between new and good second-hand clothes himself.

'Fair play to you Siobhán for buying second-hand clothes, someone else's cast offs – Mam would be delighted with her frugal daughter!'

'I wouldn't go anywhere near them at home in Galway,' she laughed. 'Sure, everybody knows everybody else there and you'd be the talk of the town. You wouldn't know whose clothes you'd be wearing! But I bet if some of those old cows could get away with buying their clothes in such shops, but not in their own town, they surely would too!'

In time, Siobhán and Abdulla became good friends. She teased him about his mad blond hair as he attempted to fit in and he took her teasing in a spirit of good humour.

He was very attentive and sympathetic and she felt comfortable talking to him about missing her home and friends. At times she wished she was working in a hotel back home, but at the same time she liked being independent and loved London.

'I guess I'm a bit mixed up still, about London,' she said, as she sat opposite Abdulla.

Some racist people had called her derogatory names like 'black papist' and told her to go back home to the land of 'spuds and cabbages'. At first she was shocked, never having heard the likes of that back in Ireland. Some ignorant English gobshites would shout things like: 'You lot didn't have spuds at one time. It's such a pity you ever got them back. We could do without the likes of you breathing our air.'

But soon Siobhán refused to take this type of abuse lying down. She gave as good as she got, almost making a fool of herself. Sometimes she couldn't believe the words coming from her own mouth. The name calling began the minute some ignorant morons heard her Irish accent. But thankfully, those people were very much in the minority. There were lots of lovely English people and she refused to be put off by the ignorance of a tiny minority. She wondered what kind of rearing they had to say such things to the Irish.

Her friend Trudy got similar treatment because she was from Scotland. Siobhán had to fight Trudy's battles for her, as she was way too timid to take on the likes of those idiots. Many a time in the hotel, Trudy was overloaded with extra work she couldn't refuse, but her friends Amahil and Siobhán tried to coach her in the art of saying 'no' without feeling guilty.

Abdulla understood exactly what Siobhán and Trudy were going through. He was also treated badly at times, but developed a thick skin in response to racist taunts, being well able to dish back insults in equal amounts.

CHAPTER 5

Siobhán falls for Abdulla's lie

When Abdulla got to know Siobhán better he began to play on her emotions. He told her he was worried about his poor mother back in Pakistan and confided in her that his father was a violent tyrant who slapped his wife around. He told her he could never go back home to this man who made everybody's life such a misery.

He had grown to love living in London. He liked his job and wanted to remain, seeing England as the place he always wanted to be. In fact, he felt like he very much belonged to what he saw as a new and sophisticated world.

Siobhán asked J.P. if he would put in a good word with the management of the hotel, to ask if Abdulla could work extra hours as he was sending money home to his mother. This was a complete lie, but Siobhán believed him.

J.P. had heard that story already and was trying to do the best he could to help Abdulla, but as a blow-in himself he wanted to avoid pushing his luck by rubbing the management up the wrong way. After all, how could he justify giving Abdulla extra hours when other staff members who were working in the hotel before Abdulla arrived also sought overtime?

She assured her brother that Abdulla and his friend Amahil worked exceptionally hard and were willing to do whatever they were asked to do in their jobs. In fact, they were determined to exceed all expectations. The management of the Royal Hotel was hard on its staff and very strict about hours, despite the fact that hard workers like them were difficult to come by. The restaurant manager never minded pushing them that bit harder and hoped they and their colleagues would grow into a strong team of workers who performed well under pressure in that busy central London hotel. Both men tried to excel throughout each busy working day and then went home to their flat when the day was done.

As far as Abdulla was concerned, it was all about keeping his head down and going for it. No matter what his boss asked of him, he was always cheerful and willing to please, answering 'No problem, sir!' with a smile on his face.

He was making good money and, along with overtime and tips from the generous hotel guests, he knew he had a bright future in London, so hard work and charm were the order of his day.

CHAPTER 6

Jim comes out

Siobhán had noticed that her cousin Jim often spoke with what she considered was a polished accent. She heard him speak like this in his workplace and when his friend Marreese was with him. His Irish accent seemed to disappear whenever he spoke to English people. It was not replaced with an 'ordinary' English accent, but with rather an affected upper-class accent that seemed to command respect with every syllable he spoke.

Jim never seemed to have a girl with him but what his cousins did notice was that he went everywhere with his friend Marreese. They appeared to be closer than brothers, but there was never a woman in sight for either of them.

J.P. and Siobhán wondered about these two good-looking fellows – surely they could both have women for company with just a click of their fingers?

The mystery was finally solved when Jim and Marreese left the siblings' flat one Monday night after having drinks and cake to mark J.P.'s birthday. Marreese had left his pink silk cravat on the couch, along with his wallet. Siobhán ran to the front door to call after them and saw them linking arms with each other with more than brotherly affection. They failed to hear Siobhán calling them so she suddenly stopped trying to get their attention. The pair carried on walking, arm in arm.

She slipped back into the flat, totally mystified at what she had seen. How was she going to tell her brother? What would the family back home think of such a thing? In her heart, Siobhán knew that she would never betray Jim by telling the family before he did, and when and if he was ever ready to tell her then she would listen and tell him that his life was his own and nobody else's bloody business!

'Pull yourself together, for God's sake!' said J.P. 'You just imagined it, Siobhán. What you saw were two very good friends who are there for each other.'

Siobhán nodded in agreement but didn't share with her brother what she really thought. She tried to convince herself that that was how good friends behaved in London, so far away from the country they had been born in. Loneliness was an awful affliction for immigrants, and people sought comfort in all sorts of ways.

Despite his initial denial, J.P. was uneasy about his cousin and felt worried about him. He knew that people attacked homosexual men all over the world. What if anything happened to Jim?

J.P. was more than a little concerned for his cousin's safety when he thought about the reality of the situation and whether his family back in Galway would accept Jim's orientation and lifestyle.

Jim had met Marreese Badeaux one Sunday afternoon in the Camden Town clothes markets by the Regent's Canal. They were both picking up the same leather jacket, holding a sleeve each over the clothes rail. Jim let go of his sleeve and apologised politely to the other man.

'No, you must have this jacket if you want it,' said Marreese.

'No, it's ok, you take it,' said Jim as he walked off casually to another clothes rail.

Marreese knew that this was not just another chance meeting. He felt this was an important encounter and he was not about to let this gorgeous dark-haired man disappear from sight.

'Excuse me,' said Marreese. 'I noticed that we both like the same kind of clothes. Are you from around here?'

'No,' Jim told him. 'I'm from Ireland, but I've been working in London now for a while.'

'Where?' asked Marreese. 'Would you like to join me for a coffee?'

A bit hesitantly, Jim agreed. He wasn't sure, but he agreed all the same. Why not, he thought. He seemed to be a nice enough man and it was only for a coffee after all.

Jim liked this tall blond-haired young man with his charming easy manner even more the minute he heard his French accent. But it was not only that – he felt a special connection, something deeper. He felt like he knew him, but it was an odd feeling, as he had never laid eyes on him before then.

Both men worked in boutiques and loved high-fashion clothes, but the attraction did not stop there. In time, they started going out to the cinema and theatre together and eventually moved into a very classy apartment and became a settled gay couple.

CHAPTER 7

Pádraig makes contact

Almost exactly a year after she left Galway, Siobhán received a letter from her former boyfriend Pádraig. He had got her address in London from a friend of hers in Ireland, and in his letter he pleaded with her to come home.

He made the invitation on the condition that she had not met someone new in London, and that she still had genuine feelings for him. He told her that he had missed her dreadfully for a long time, but he had deliberately not contacted her until now as he wrote, tongue-in-cheek, that she might already have met someone over there with plenty of money and a big house. He told her he was still working in the hardware shop and had little to offer her at the moment but he was going to night classes, studying to become an architectural draughtsman, with a view to eventually qualifying as an architect, stating that as the reason why he had not followed her over to London.

Siobhán was immediately overcome with emotion when she read his letter and knew at once what she wanted from life, realising it was to be with this man. So she made up her mind to return to her sweetheart, the love of her life, as it seemed he was finally ready to make a firm commitment, even if it had taken her move to London to make him fully appreciate her and to take this bold initiative.

She always felt she had left her heart back home in Galway. Life was good in London but she would have no problem leaving it behind her. Oh, the excitement of it all! With more than a few pounds in her back pocket, she hoped to start up a small confectionary café at home, but in the meantime she could try to get a job in the Salthill Hotel in Galway to make up the shortfall in her finances.

Siobhán knew that she would miss her life in London, and everything about it, especially the many wonderful people she had met, including her friend Trudy. Her name was short for Gertrude, she had bright red curls and a few tiny freckles on the tip of her nose. Trudy always seemed to be nodding her head in agreement with everyone – as if she had no opinion about anything herself. She was so caring and giving to everyone in the hotel but she was bullied constantly because others saw her as an easy target. Siobhán had taken her under her protective wing and worried for her and kept telling her repeatedly to stand up for herself. But Trudy would just stammer out submissive words in her meek little way, always apologising and letting others dominate her.

Tears welled up in Siobhán's eyes at the prospect of leaving Trudy, but she knew that she couldn't always be there to encourage this most timid of souls. She felt bad leaving her to the wolves and hoped that Amahil would be there for her. The girl was used and abused for her unlimited kindness, always taking a back seat to accommodate the wishes of others. Siobhán fervently hoped that wisdom would prevail and that Trudy would finally exert herself and sort out all those lousy insincere people on her own, while standing up for herself and her beliefs.

Just before Siobhán left for home she asked Amahil if he would keep an eye on Trudy because she knew that she and the gentle Pakistani man got on very well. She also hoped that Trudy would eventually meet a decent man, someone like her Pádraig.

Exactly one month after Pádraig's letter arrived, she was packed and ready to go back home. She said goodbye to Abdulla; he had become a close friend and was upset to see her leave London for Galway. Her boss Ruth was also upset at losing a good worker but she wished her well, glad she was achieving her dream of getting married. She even gave her extra money in her final pay cheque to show her appreciation for all the hard work that Siobhán had put into her job at the hotel – always with a smile and eager to please.

Jim and Marreese met up with J.P. and Siobhán at Heathrow Airport to see her off on her flight back to Dublin. After tea and chat in the departure lounge, she was ready to check in. She waved goodbye and blew a kiss and then she was gone, heading towards a new life back home with Pádraig.

When Siobhán came through arrivals at Dublin Airport she could see him from a distance, recognising his tall frame and distinctive dark curly hair. Pádraig was dressed in a dark grey formal suit, the first time she had ever seen him dress up like that. He was standing there waiting for her, with a tender, expectant look in his dark eyes. Both of them tried to speak at the same time, feeling both nervous and excited.

At last Siobhán said with a giggle, 'Now. Let's start again.'

She told him how much she had missed him and how wonderful it was to be home and back with him again.

Pádraig immediately took a black and gold box from his breast pocket. Inside was an engagement ring, gold with a gorgeous diamond setting. There and then in the arrivals hall of Dublin Airport he proposed, gently asking Siobhán to marry him, while dropping down on one knee. He could not wait to ask her parents. He knew she loved him – after all, that was why she had given up so much in London to come back to him – so he felt he knew what her answer would be. She immediately said yes and the young couple sealed their engagement with a passionate kiss, thrilled to be starting an exciting future together. The pair had attracted the attention of some amused onlookers who applauded their touching proposal scene.

Back in London, J.P. felt a huge loss without his sister. He missed her around the flat, which felt empty without her clothes drying on the backs of chairs, or her bits and pieces around the place. But most of all he missed the sound of her voice and her cheerful company. He always felt more Irish when the two were together, but now a feeling of intense loneliness had descended on him without her around. He had settled in well to life in London and was happy with every aspect of his new life, but it took a while for the sadness to leave him as he found himself feeling empty and alone.

J.P. asked Jim to accompany him to discos and parties at weekends after Siobhán left, always hoping that his cousin would find a girl to share his life. But Marreese always arrived at some point and came home with the two Irishmen.

J.P. knew that Jim's love life was none of his business and that what he did with it was up to him. Jim had been exceptionally kind and helpful to him and his sister, but he was sad at the thought that Jim might never have children of his own, feeling somehow that Jim's fast and indulgent lifestyle was getting in the way of his future happiness.

And what was J.P. thinking deep down about Jim's own choice in life? Did he think it was acceptable? Somehow, he felt a faint disapproval. Even though it was the late twentieth *century, there was still a long way to go*, thought J.P., before any kind of true equality would be accepted by society.

CHAPTER 8

Siobhán's happiness is shattered

Siobhán got a call from her fiancé Pádraig early on a Saturday morning the following summer, saying he needed to talk to her urgently. Her heart seemed to miss a beat as she reacted to the tone of his voice.

'Tell me, is everything ok love?' she asked anxiously, sensing that all might not be well. But he refused to answer her question.

Maybe he was planning a picnic she wondered? After all, it was a beautiful warm August day and if he gave any details the surprise would be spoiled. But she quickly rejected that notion. She asked if ten o'clock would be alright to meet him, to which he immediately agreed.

Siobhán hung up and went over to her wardrobe to put out a white tee-shirt, a pair of red shorts she had bought in London and a pair of white runners. After a shower, she dressed and tied up her wet hair and then made a quick bolt for the door, shouting to her mother that she would be back later on.

She met Pádraig inside the gates of the local park, sensing the smell of freshly cut grass and the perfume of summer flowers as she approached him. She was trying to take in what Pádraig was saying to her but all she could hear was a buzzing in her ears and a creeping sense of dread. She pulled herself together and tried to pay more attention to the words he was saying. He was clearly upset and looked like he had not slept for days.

'What do you mean you want to break off our engagement? Is there someone else?' stammered Siobhán, fearful of his answer.

'No, of course not,' said Pádraig.

She felt dizzy and sick. But apparently he had a serious problem, and it centred around her parents. He said they didn't think he was good enough for her – after all, he only worked in the co-op, and had few career prospects.

'Say that again, Pádraig,' she said, not quite catching his meaning.

Pádraig had overheard a conversation between Siobhán's father and his own boss in the co-op. They had been discussing Pádraig's potential earnings, and his future with Siobhán. Neither man had noticed the presence of Pádraig, who was standing within earshot, behind some cans of paint.

'Your father told my boss that maybe you could do a lot better than me. He hoped you'd see sense and make no rash decisions.'

Pádraig told her he was not going to be thought of as second class by the likes of her parents.

'Do you hear what I'm saying Siobhán? Keep the ring – do whatever you want with it. I'm not prepared to go on with that sort of attitude from your family,' he said in indignation and frustration.

'Why didn't you tell them that you were studying to become an architect?' she asked. 'Would that not have made any difference to their tiny little minds?'

'No, my boss surely would have fired me on the spot, saying that I was not really interested in working there,' said Pádraig. He began to walk away with tears in his eyes and obviously appeared very hurt and vulnerable.

He half blamed himself and wished he had stayed on at school. But he had had no choice in the matter, having been pulled out of school out of dire necessity to help his struggling family. Under different circumstances, he could by now have been qualified for the job of his dreams. Early in his working life, he had whiled away most of his evenings telling jokes and playing snooker after a hard day at work before he copped on to himself and made the life-changing decision to go back to education. He knew it would change everything and was a vital investment in a better future. But he felt the joke was now on him to be thought of as worthless by those people. Pádraig could not decide if he was angry at Siobhán's parents or his parents or even at himself for the way things had turned out, but it was all too much for him and he couldn't hold back the tears any longer.

'Hold on a minute,' Siobhán cried after him as he walked away. 'Alright then, but you can have your ring back – sure, why would I want it now?' She pulled the ring roughly off her finger and fired it at him, not caring if it got lost in the grass. It didn't matter anymore she felt, as she began to scream angrily at him. She had known her parents were not fond of Pádraig, and certainly they worried about his job prospects, but she had believed that in time he would be fully accepted into the O'Rourke household.

Despite her angry gesture of throwing the ring back, she felt that Pádraig *had been over-sensitive and had overreacted to something he wasn't meant to hear.* She tried to convince herself that he just needed to cool down and then he would come back to her.

She could see why her father would be worried for her – after all, Padraig's salary did not amount to very much. Even with both of them earning, they would still be struggling if they wanted to buy their own home and begin married life together. It would take some years for him to receive his qualification and transform his future. Even so, her father had no business meddling in her life at this time, just as she had found a path to future happiness.

But Pádraig was not to be consoled. He was adamant and insisted through his bitter tears that he could see no future for them together.

Siobhán was heartbroken and filled with a deep anger, feeling completely betrayed by the people she thought she loved most.

CHAPTER 9

Abdulla comes back on the scene

When Pádraig had not contacted Siobhán for a full week after their bitter confrontation in the local park, she rang her friend Abdulla in London and poured out all her feelings of heartbreak and misery to him. They had been good friends when she was over there and she felt she could talk to him and ask his advice. She was glad that she had kept in touch with him by phone since she returned to Ireland.

Abdulla had cultivated some contacts down in County Cork and had made up his mind that he was going to leave his job in London and come to Ireland. There would be a lot more at stake if he failed to make the move now, so he quit his job, having made plans for a better life in a new place. Because of his friendship with J.P. and Siobhán, he already felt he knew quite a lot about life in Ireland and he felt the slower pace of life would suit him very well.

He told his boss he had a family member in Ireland who was dying of cancer and he had to go and help the family out because most of the poor man's relatives were back home in Pakistan. His boss immediately gave him a good reference and some extra money for being such an exceptional worker. He told him he was sorry to see him go and that if his plans in Ireland didn't work out, he would be glad to give him a job back in the hotel as a commis chef at any time.

Two weeks after Siobhán called him, Abdulla made his way to Dublin. He was afraid to leave it any longer in case she got back with her former fiancé. In doing so, he was hoping that he would receive a favourable reception from the sister of his former colleague.

Arriving in Dun Laoghaire Harbour from Galway on a blustery September day, Siobhán desperately tried to hold her hair in place, believing she would look a holy show if she couldn't find a few hair clips in her handbag to keep things in place. The ship had already docked. She was very pleased to see Abdulla's familiar face as he made his way over to her and put his arms gently around her shoulders like a dear friend.

'You said that you would fill me in on everything when I arrived in Dublin,' said Abdulla, who was delighted to see his close friend again.

'Why did you decide to come by sea instead of flying?' asked Siobhán.

'To tell you the truth, I made a good saving by travelling by sea, so I didn't mind the extra time it took me to get over here,' he said warmly, smiling broadly at Siobhán.

He filled her in on everything that was happening back in London and told her how well J.P. was looking, and she in turn told him the story about Pádraig and the sad ending of the engagement, from start to finish. This all took place before they had even left the docking platform.

They then made their way over to a local café and ordered a couple of teas. Siobhán couldn't help herself and started to cry again. Her world was falling apart – what was she going to do? She felt she still loved Pádraig very much. They were childhood sweethearts and she had always believed they would marry when the time was right. She also recalled the terrible row with her mother that followed the news of the breakup.

'How did I read Pádraig so wrong, Abdulla? How am I going to get through this? You're a good friend, please, tell me. Please Abdulla, would you mind staying around for a while before you go to Cork?'

'Siobhán, don't you worry at all. Everything will work out in the end.'

He had hatched a devious plan, knowing he must be very careful so that she would not suspect anything.

'Are you sure his mind is made up, and is there no going back to your life with him?' He watched her closely, gauging her reaction. 'Has he tried to contact you?'

'No.'

'Well, there's your answer! Do you think it would help you to get over this heartbreak by having me, your friend, close by your side?'

Siobhán was not quite sure what he was getting at. He was her friend indeed, but she was slightly taken aback at such a suggestion, suspecting that Abdulla might harbour serious feelings for her.

'Look Siobhán, I don't mean to be too direct about this, but if I could be a deep source of comfort to you at this very difficult time, I would be happy to step in and look after you.' He again placed his hand gently on her shoulder.

'But if you're not ready to start a new life, well ...' He wasn't sure of himself and found it difficult to explain how he really felt.

Siobhán certainly wasn't sure of anything anymore, so she just looked directly at this gentle and sympathetic man, feeling more confused than ever.

'We get on well, don't we, Siobhán?' said Abdulla, knowing that he was moving way too fast and he must slow down for his own sake. He wanted to avoid frightening her. If that happened, she would be gone forever out of his life.

'We're able to talk to each other about everything, isn't that true, Siobhán?'

He told her he knew she liked him as a good friend, and that was fine, but he seemed to be suggesting that there might be a possibility to explore a heightening of that relationship.

'Look, Siobhán, Pádraig made it clear to you that your engagement is over, so you can't go back grovelling to the likes of him. In his heart, he could not have cared for you the way he said he did, being swayed entirely by what other people thought of your relationship, rather than being sure of his love for you. You're far too good for that kind of rubbish, Siobhán. Trust me, please. I would dearly love to take good care of you now and help you to get over this awful time.'

He drew her closer to him, giving her a long, comforting hug.

She was truly delighted to see him, and that meant she cared for him as a true friend, but that was a very different feeling to the love she had for Pádraig. But now she felt drawn to this gentle, caring man and she felt very grateful for his support, his charm and his sincerity. But she felt she might be taking a big gamble with her life, as she put her past behind her, snuggling in closer to the warm embrace of this caring friend.

Siobhán rang J.P. from a phone box outside the small café and asked him his opinion on what she should do, explaining how Abdulla had approached her as she tried to deal with her difficult situation. But J.P. said he was not sure at all about Abdulla being the man for his sister. He thought for a moment and told her that he felt she should stick with her own kind.

'I know he's a good and kind man, but you are cultures apart. He might never understand our traditions at all Siobhán and you might never understand his.'

Siobhán listened to her brother's words of caution but somehow she could sense a gradual change of emotion, being mysteriously drawn to the exotic appeal of Abdulla. They were the best of friends. She got on so well with him and her friends in London felt he was a decent, caring man who would always stand by a woman who made a commitment to him.

Abdulla had first seen Siobhán when he was out for a night with her brother in London and was immediately drawn to her, both in terms of her looks and her easy manner. He remembered how Siobhán had been so homesick at first, and he was always there to ask her if he could be of any help to make her feel better. He was very taken by her exceptional attractiveness and wondered if she might be the one for him. But he never gave her any clue about his real feelings. He felt she could play a big part in his plan to stay in London, which he was desperate to do – he knew that if he went back home to his own country, his father would insist on him marrying a nice local Muslim girl, one of his own kind.

Abdulla had known that he must take things slowly and not push himself towards Siobhán too soon, realising the reality of the cultural and racial differences that could stand in the way of making a life together in the future. So he had decided to play his cards right and exercise extreme patience during the time Siobhán lived in London. But then Pádraig, her boyfriend back home, had appeared from nowhere and pledged his undying love for her, and she had suddenly gone home to Ireland! That unexpected turn of events had upset all his future plans.

When she left, Abdulla thought he would never see her again, but now her misfortune had fallen right into his lap and presented him with an opportunity to change his life. Now he was back on track because of this unexpected second chance that had come his way. A lot was riding on this big gamble about coming to Ireland and he hoped it would finally pay off in his favour.

Abdulla told Siobhán about the situation down in County Cork, and that he had arranged for them both to visit his family there.

'What do you think, Siobhán? This will be an ideal chance to get as far away from your angry parents in Galway as soon as possible – and of course, it will give you time to put space between you and the man who changed your happiness into misery. Maybe it's time to make a fresh start! Do you think that would be a good idea Siobhan?'

Abdulla could see a good life ahead for both of them if he could persuade her to marry him, taking up where the other man had let her down.

CHAPTER 10

Marriage in London and elopement to Cork

Things were moving at a dizzying pace for Siobhán. She took the train from Galway into Dublin. Here she was now, agreeing to go to Cork with her friend Abdulla – a trip she had not anticipated, with a man who was just a friend. It was a change of direction that presented itself without any warning and certainly no preparation.

First, she would have to go back to Galway to her parents' house to get some clothes and whatever she would need to bring with her to Cork. She needed some time to think, to try to deal with the enormity of the situation she suddenly found herself in.

She liked Abdulla a lot. She found him attractive, sensitive and honourable – but that was as far as it went. She certainly did not feel in love with him. It seemed to her that his feelings were much more intense and she was not sure how to cope with that. It appeared that Abdulla had a vision of them sharing a life together, which was not something she had foreseen. It also seemed that the Cork trip was more than just a visit to a sick friend and that Abdulla saw it as a new start, one that included her. Apart from her unresolved feelings, there were important practical issues to be looked after.

She had been lucky enough to get her old job back in Galway when she returned from London. Did Abdulla feel she could just throw all that up to be with him in Cork, a place she had never been to before?

When she raised these issues with Abdulla he offered her immediate reassurance. 'Siobhán, you don't need to worry about money. I have enough money to buy more clothes and to look after both of us.'

He pulled out a large wad of English notes from his smart navy jacket to back up what he said.

'Look, you can buy all the clothes that you need. And you can write to your employer at the hotel in Galway about your job. Just explain that your life has taken a sudden turn and that you are unable to continue living in Galway for personal reasons.'

As he said all this he knew that if he let her go now, there was a big chance that she and Pádraig might get back together and then all his chances with Siobhán would come to nothing.

Siobhán wondered what her parents would say if they knew there was a plan to run off with a stranger, a Pakistani man they had never met. How could she live with that? she thought. She felt a shiver pass through her whole body, as if someone was walking on her grave, but she put it all at the back of her mind for now.

What was she to do? Abdulla could see she was worried and upset due to her inner turmoil. He pulled her close to him.

'Look Siobhán, you can trust me. I will take care of you,' he said tenderly. He assured her he wanted to take her away from all the heartache, and away from Galway, with all its painful reminders of Pádraig and the way he had treated her. As he talked, he gently stroked her fine blonde hair, pulling her even closer to him.

Siobhán slowly began to feel reassured. Here was a man she and her brother had known well in London. He was a decent and trustworthy person and he sounded like he had her best interests at heart. Feeling a wave of emotion, she put her arms around her strong friend and cautiously yielded to his advances.

They then drove to a small garage in Dun Laoghaire to look for some sort of transport for Abdulla, who wanted a vehicle of his own. The salesman offered a second-hand blue Toyota van. Abdulla was delighted with it but did not let the salesman see that. After much haggling over the price of the van, a deal was struck between them and everything agreed. Abdulla was free to drive the van away, after insuring it and using his driving licence from the United Kingdom.

So Abdulla and Siobhán were on their way down to County Cork to his relatives there – or so she thought.

It took a month for Pádraig to cool down and to think rationally about the breakup. Clearly having second thoughts, he called at Siobhán's workplace to ask her to forgive him for what he had put her through. But her former boss told him that Siobhán had suddenly left the hotel without working out her notice and it seemed she had left Galway also.

Pádraig also asked her friend Marie if she knew anything about her whereabouts, but she had no idea either. Marie had gone over to Siobhán's worried parents and they had told her that it was completely unlike their daughter to just disappear. They admitted there had been harsh words said about the engagement row but would say no more.

When they arrived in Cork, Abdulla bought the *Cork Evening Echo* to look for houses to rent in the county. Siobhán spotted a notice for a small cottage in the grounds of an old country farmhouse in a rural area not far from the city.

The couple made their way to the estate and drove straight into the courtyard. They rang the bell on the door of the house to inquire if the cottage was still available.

As they waited for an answer, Siobhán clenched her fists and prayed silently before the door opened. *'Please, please like the look of us and if you don't I will take it as a sign that I shouldn't be here and I'll make my way straight back to Galway.'*

She anticipated their future with mixed emotions, still feeling the pain of the breakup with Pádraig. He had let her down very badly, just because he could not accept what her parents really thought of him. He had not even put up a fight for her! She would have gone to the ends of the earth for him, he knew that. It seemed like he must not really have loved her at all, giving in to parental disapproval so easily.

'The pair of you are in luck. It's still available for rent,' said Albert Herbert after checking with his wife Julie. They were the owners of the country house on Burrow Hill, nestled in the quiet countryside of County Cork.

Feeling more secure, Siobhán began to have feelings of stronger attraction to the gentle and charming man she was with. In time, things became more physical and she became secure enough to feel she could sleep with him. She believed Abdulla really loved her and she had always found him to be a very attractive and sincere man.

Abdulla lost no time in his efforts to formalise their relationship. Following a number of long and sometimes heated discussions, they decided to get married, as Siobhán's feelings for Pádraig dissolved into the past. They felt there might be too many problems trying to get married in 1970s Ireland, so they opted for London instead, a place where they both felt at home in the multicultural atmosphere of that city.

It took a couple of weeks to set a date and arrange a registry office wedding. Finally, they were on their way to get married in Camden Registry Office. Abdulla asked Siobhán not to mention the wedding to her brother as he thought it would be much more intimate with just the two of them – and besides, J.P. probably would have wanted their family to come over from Galway and Abdulla felt that would not have worked, as they had not even been told about the relationship, let alone their wedding plans. Besides, the idea of a Catholic girl from Galway marrying a Muslim man from Lahore would almost certainly have been too much for them to take. Abdulla was also afraid that J.P. would talk her out of marrying in such haste.

For her wedding, Siobhán wore a knee-length cream dress and carried a small bunch of gypsophila. Abdulla was dressed in a smart black suit with a cream tie to match Siobhán's dress, and he still sported his blond highlights.

Siobhán thought he looked even more handsome than the first time she had met him, although she was never sure about his blond hair – she had to admit to herself that it looked strange against his very dark skin tone and his natural black hair was more appropriate.

They spent their wedding night in one of the posher hotels in London and the next day Abdulla took his new wife to the mosque off Holloway Road.

'I need to introduce you to my Muslim roots Siobhán, to show you a little about my faith.'

Siobhán looked around her as they made their way up the steps of the mosque. She noticed that all the women had their heads covered as they walked into the mosque. Abdulla handed her a brown silk scarf with a smile, saying she must put it on her head before they entered that holy place.

She felt uneasy about the mosque, but told herself not to read too much into something that did not affect her at all – and what was this scarf all about anyway? After looking around at all the women with covered heads, she looked at her husband directly. She reminded him that he had told her that all this religious stuff was behind him when he lived in London, so why was he suddenly becoming so keen now?

'You know that I am a Catholic girl, this religion is not for me, Abdulla.'

'Siobhán, I learned that the women in Ireland, your own country, wore head scarfs in the 1950s and 60s to go to Mass, so what are you afraid of now my darling?'

It should have been the happiest time of her life but, all of a sudden, coming out of the mosque, she felt a heavy cloud descend over her, having looked at all those people praying and chanting – a totally different tradition from her upbringing in Catholicism.

Why was she so worried? A voice in her head told her she should be worried. She thought for a mad moment that she wanted to run back down to the registrar who had married them, to ask him to cancel this marriage, because she felt she had made a big mistake. But her legs refused to take her back in the direction of the registry office. Abdulla had complained to her many a time about his upbringing when they both worked in England, and not ever wanting to go back to his father's way of life or their Muslim faith. Now Siobhán felt trapped, but why did she feel that way? She wondered if he could practise his faith independently of hers, but something in the back of her mind told her a different story.

Now all Abdulla had to do was wait for her to become pregnant – and he would do his damndest to make sure it happened, supplying her with plenty of brandy and smooth talking.

Back in County Cork, the weeks passed and the owners and tenants of the house got on well. The Herberts did not see much of Abdulla, but he assured them there would be no problems with paying the rent on the first day of every month.

He had already explained to the Herberts that he was working full-time with Pakistani relatives who had set up a business in Clonakilty, so all was good. However, Siobhán still had strong reservations about their relationship.

Around that time, a very concerned Pádraig travelled over to England to look for Siobhán. Her friend Marie had given him J.P.'s address. His boss gave him a week off work but told him it must come out of his holiday entitlement.

He turned up at the flat thinking that Siobhán would be there and most probably would have got her old job back. Siobhan's family and friends assumed the same thing. He waited and waited for one of them to come back to the flat.

J.P. finally arrived to find Pádraig waiting outside; Pádraig was shocked to find out from her brother that Siobhán had never gone over to England at all.

J.P. could not bring himself to tell Pádraig about the worrying phone call he had got from his sister, telling him the truth.

The next day, Pádraig made his way back home, feeling both confused and depressed, while deeply worried about the woman he had loved for so long.

CHAPTER 11

Abdulla tightens his grip

As time went on, Siobhán saw to her horror that she had made a terrible mistake by marrying her former friend Abdulla. Although he appeared to be a charming man to the many people he came into contact with, he was increasingly showing his true colours on a domestic level. She knew in her heart that she should have trusted her instinct when she experienced a sense of serious doubt about marrying him the minute she stepped into the registry office in London. She should have returned to Dublin immediately and gone back to her job and her family in her beloved Galway.

There were many questions she kept asking herself. Why did she go through with the marriage ceremony? How did she fall for this charmer? Did she really feel she loved him? He had been a great friend in a different life and she had found it easy to like him when she lived in London. But now he was so different towards her and she realised that she *was facing a life with a stranger she had absolutely nothing in common with. Why had she just abandoned her family and her friend Marie, back in Galway?* As an educated woman, she should have known better, rather than showing such poor judgement of character. Being a friend of Abdulla's was one thing, but being his wife was an entirely different matter. It was becoming increasingly obvious that Muslim men like Abdulla saw their wives in a totally different role to the men she knew in Ireland, and he expected her to play a role which filled her with revulsion.

Siobhán took a job as a cook in Mackey's, a small local hotel. Her hours were from 7.30 a.m. until 5.30 p.m., five days a week. As married life continued, some harsh realities about the type of man Abdulla really was became depressingly clear.

She tried to ignore her worries, but they would not go away. For a start, Abdulla expected a lot of sex. At first, she thought it was just an extended sort of honeymoon affair, but as the months went on, he demanded more and was very forceful with her. This was not normal sexual relations between man and wife, it was forceful and violent and she often suffered both mentally and physically.

Siobhán had nobody to discuss his behaviour with, so she had to suffer alone. She could not confide in anyone at her workplace as she did not know the local people well enough. She found her freedom being restricted more and more in a very sinister way.

One evening when she tried to relax by reading some popular women's magazines Abdulla became angry and told her that such magazines were complete rubbish and not suitable to have in the house. At first she thought he wasn't serious, but it became obvious that he held a very different view about what was suitable reading for a woman, including his wife. This irrational curbing of her limited freedom shocked her and caused her to worry even more.

Everything changed when she found out she was pregnant. Abdulla knew he then had her exactly where he wanted her, because she was carrying his child. His sense of control and ownership put Siobhán in a very dangerous place at a time when a woman should be very happy at the prospect of becoming a first-time mother.

After the magazine episode, he struck another blow to Siobhán's confidence as a woman when he objected violently to her use of makeup.

'You don't need to put that rubbish on your face anymore,' he told her. He grabbed her in a rage and commanded that she take it off at once. He even went as far as trying to remove her makeup himself with a cloth from the sink. She was absolutely stunned at his monstrous actions, unable to believe what this man felt he could do in terms of curbing her freedom as a woman.

'And you must also remove that nail varnish from your fingernails and your toenails.'

He spat out these vicious commands like a man possessed and poor Siobhán was too frightened to disobey the commands of a man who was clearly created in the same mould as his demon father back in Lahore. Having stood up to his tyrant of a father as a younger man, he was now developing into the same sort of beast himself – brutal, controlling and prone to practising exactly the same sort of violence his poor mother had suffered.

Siobhán was four months pregnant when she rang her parents to apologise for eloping – all over a stupid row with them. She thought back to the last conversation they had. It was not simply a stupid row. They had explained that they felt Pádraig did not have anything much to offer their daughter in the way of a good life, despite her feelings for him. They did not want to see her living in hardship, so he was not going to be accepted by them under any circumstances. He had no career and no background worth talking about.

'He's not one of us! Do you hear us, Siobhán? For God's sake, listen,' her father had insisted. Her parents had hoped that she would have seen that for herself and it was unfortunate that Pádraig had heard her father and his boss discussing his job prospects in his workplace, her very upset mother told her.

Those were the last words she had heard as she stormed out of her parents' house. She had stayed with her friend Marie for a couple of weeks, and then she rang Abdulla crying on the phone. He was delighted because he at once saw a door of opportunity opening for him!

With her eyes filling with tears she asked herself why she had not eloped with Pádraig instead, dismissing what people had said in

Galway. She would have gone to Australia, or America or Canada or anywhere in the world with him if only he had not been so pig-headed about the attitude of her parents. Who knows, he could have qualified as an architect, worked hard and they could have had a wonderful life together. And they could have returned triumphantly to Ireland to show her parents that they were wrong about the man she loved.

Siobhán often thought back to when she had first met Abdulla in London with her brother. He appeared to be a true gentleman who had become broken and vulnerable after suffering at the hands of his father. He often told her stories about growing up in Pakistan under such oppression, and how it had hardened his resolve to escape to something better, free to live as he wished.

One Wednesday night on the phone, she told Liam and Bridget the whole sorry story from start to finish. She knew she had brought all this on herself, she told them, but she said they also had to take some of the blame. They were partly responsible for Pádraig's actions through their rejection of him. They told her they were worried sick about her and begged her to come home, to make a fresh start. But she felt she could not do that, knowing that she was expecting Abdulla's child – and besides, how could she ever face Pádraig again? But they insisted that they had to see her and they planned to visit her in County Cork very soon.

On Easter Sunday morning, Siobhán was out on the street with some of her work colleagues when she spotted Julie, her landlady, coming out of the local Church of Ireland church. Siobhán made her way over to her to wish her a happy Easter and Julie touched her hand warmly, asking if she was alright. Surprised to be asked that question, Siobhán asked her what she meant. Julie explained that she had heard noise coming from the cottage a couple of nights before and she wondered if all was well on the domestic front.

Siobhán lied to her, assuring Julie that everything was fine.

'Well glad to hear that all is good with you Siobhán. And how is your husband Abdulla settling here in Ireland?'

Siobhán felt she had to give a positive response, not wanting to draw attention to the marital disharmony she was living through. Her response was immediate and she tried to reassure Julie that Abdulla was fine, that he loved Ireland and the slow pace of life. She added that he was working long hours and by the time he got home he was often exhausted and could sometimes become irritated with small things.

Although Julie had initially welcomed both Siobhan and Abdulla as a couple, she was beginning to have reservations about him. She couldn't put her finger on it, but she felt that all was not well with this man, and she was developing a strong dislike of him.

'I'm having a few friends over for afternoon tea today Siobhán and you are very welcome to join us. Would you like that?'

The invitation was pointedly made only to Siobhán and did not include Abdulla.

'I'd be delighted to join you,' said Siobhán. She was pleased to be invited … it gave her a tremendous boost and lifted her spirits, making her feel more alive than she had felt in a very long time.

Siobhán looked longingly down the street at the local Roman Catholic church, its grey granite spire picked out in the afternoon sunlight. At that moment, she wished she was living as a good Catholic. She missed the reassurance of being part of a community, sharing in the life of a parish. She felt a certain guilt, sorry that she had neglected going to Mass and sharing in the sacraments of the Church. The loss of all that caused her much pain, which manifested itself as a physical pain in her chest. The more she thought about it, the more unbearable it became. She had lost her freedom … her way of life. Here she was in her own country, tied to the wishes of an oppressive and fanatical man from a totally different culture, one that was totally alien to hers.

She waved goodbye to Julie, thanking her for the invitation and yearning to tell her the bitter truth, but she felt that such a course of action was not open to her.

'I have only myself to blame,' she thought. She had told herself that many a time, but at the same time, surely she had an advantage being in her own country – there had to be a way out.

Siobhán's worried parents left Galway and travelled to County Cork three weeks later to try to help their troubled daughter. Abdulla would not allow them to stay in the cottage, fearing that his hold over her might be lessened in some way by being in close contact with her parents. Like any Irish parents, they assumed they would be welcomed into the home of their daughter, but this was no normal situation. Abdulla was showing signs of a split personality. Part of his cultural orientation was to share family values, but this visit reinforced his desire to dominate his wife away from the influence of her family, and having her away from their influence was what he wanted to ensure.

Siobhán asked Julie if her parents could stay in her house for one night. She knew her request might have sounded a little strange and that it could result in rejection, but fortunately Julie recognised that the cottage was too small for guests to stay, and her suspicions were not aroused.

'Don't worry Siobhán. I know the house is very small. Let me ask Albert if we can put them up in one of our spare rooms.'

Albert was strict about strangers staying in their home and Julie knew she might unfortunately have to offer an apology to Siobhán. In the end, it was agreed that Siobhán's parents would stay with their housekeeper in the gate-lodge for one night. Siobhán was relieved to be able to have her loving parents close by, without incurring the anger of her husband.

'Thank you so much Julie. I will never be able to repay your kindness. It means a lot to me and to my parents to be able to stay here.'

Her eyes filled with tears of gratitude for Julie, but how was she to know the truth – that Siobhán was becoming increasingly terrified of Abdulla but could not bring herself to tell her the truth – Siobhan could hardly believe it herself. She was once such an independent woman.

Abdulla refused to meet her parents, which amounted to the most incredible act of rudeness and ignorance. He had no desire to meet her parents and Siobhán knew that Abdulla desperately wanted to avoid answering any questions her father might ask. The man was a despicable coward and his actions deeply affected his wife, knowing how much they wanted to share in the life of their daughter, especially now that she was pregnant.

He tried to make excuses to cover up his true motivations. 'Siobhán, where could we put them up in this tiny house? I'm sure your mum and dad will understand.'

'You needn't worry. Julie is putting them up in the gate-lodge. Mrs Murphy has no problem with this arrangement for one night,' said Siobhán, fighting back her tears.

The following day, Siobhán took her parents out to lunch in the hotel where she worked. Liam had no problem making his feelings clear about Abdulla. 'What sort of man is this? He is now my son-in-law and he refuses to see me. You know I am totally insulted and I don't want to insult him back, but he seems to be a total ignoramus to me. How dare he treat you and your mother like this?'

Siobhán was completely devastated by events, but she was still very glad to see her parents, so she tried to make light of her husband's behaviour. Her mother was also very upset and mystified. 'I don't know how people behave in Pakistan, but I'm sure this sort of carry-on cannot be normal.'

That evening, Siobhán waved them off on their way to Galway

with a heavy heart, knowing that worse was to come with the man who called himself her husband.

The next day, Abdulla stepped up his campaign of brutality against his gentle Irish wife. She wore a gold chain and cross her mother had given to her on her 18th birthday. Abdulla just pulled it roughly from her neck, breaking the chain and damaging the cross. Not only was this a Christian symbol that he would not tolerate, but he forbade his wife to wear any sort of jewellery. He was consumed with anger, not wanting his wife to show any sign of femininity or decoration by wearing jewellery of any description in 'his house'.

'His house,' thought Siobhán, who was working hard to pay her share of the rent. 'Put a beggar on horseback and he will ride straight to hell.' This was the path Abdulla was on, she thought.

The words echoed again and again in Siobhán's mind when she thought of this new act of what amounted to terror, being committed on her by the man she was beginning to despise more and more.

Siobhán first felt the force of her husband's wrath when she returned from Mass one Sunday. After all, she was a Catholic and wanted to practise her faith in complete freedom. She had told him that in the mosque in London the day they were married. She had not been inside a church for a long time and was feeling very guilty about that. In the church, she had lit a candle and prayed to St Jude, the patron saint for hopeless cases. In doing so, she hoped her prayers would be answered in her favour. She needed to ask God for forgiveness for being so gullible and she prayed that Abdulla would treat her with love and respect.

She knew she should not be afraid of Abdulla and she felt she should stand up to him. But that day she behaved like her timid friend Trudy, back in England, and he showed his true character. She wished she had a friend to defend her, like she had been for Trudy. But deep down she had a fear of what her husband was capable of doing. So she felt she was right to be on her guard.

'Where have you been,' he demanded of her.

'What do you mean?' she answered. 'I have been to Mass, as all Catholics do on a Sunday.'

'You're a married woman now and you're married to me,' he roared, shaking with anger. 'Don't you realise you are married to a Muslim man? So that makes you a Muslim woman in my eyes, and you must behave like a good Muslim wife.'

'No, I am still a Catholic. I have not converted to your religious faith and I do not intend to,' protested Siobhán, becoming tearful and intimidated by this domineering maniac of a husband.

'Now you can leave all that Mass rubbish behind you,' he bellowed, pressing his hands down hard on her shoulders. 'There will be no more Mass and rosaries for you, Siobhán. You are my wife and it is my duty to teach you the Quran and to let you know about the true revelations of God. From now on, you must dress like a good Muslim woman and you will obey me in every way. Do you understand me?'

Siobhán was beginning to feel dizzy with all this violent and irrational behaviour from her husband. Her head began to buzz and she was becoming disorientated, and terrified, just as he wanted her to feel. She was beginning to suffer her first panic attack – a sudden unreasonable feeling of fear and anxiety, with the classic symptoms of a racing heart, fast breathing and sweating.

But things descended to a truly horrible level when Abdulla suddenly hit her a glancing blow to the head, causing her to be almost paralysed with fear. She ran from the kitchen to the bedroom and lay there in tears, wondering what worse things could be in store, now that she had been physically assaulted as a pregnant woman.

Away from home, Abdulla was acting the role of his father, even though he despised him, as well as having turned his back on his own religious beliefs. In his head, he could not get away from his roots, his family or their beliefs, which he had once vowed to leave behind forever. It was ingrained in his DNA and like many a son who had been abused by his father, he found himself taking on the same role.

Siobhán was his wife now and he wanted her to do his bidding at all times. It did not matter to him if she was Irish and Catholic. In his mind, she was legally his wife and he felt quite justified in dominating every aspect of her existence. She should be at his beck and call, no matter what.

He went to the bedroom and demanded sex from the woman he had just assaulted and treated with utter contempt. She was too frightened to resist and what followed constituted rape within marriage.

Part of his possessiveness stemmed from a belief that Siobhán belonged to him and he was determined that no other man should ever look at her. She was his personal property and he felt he could treat her any way he saw fit. That included regular physical assaults like the one he had committed that day in response to her attempt to practise her Catholic faith.

CHAPTER 12

Siobhán attempts to break for freedom

Monday morning came and Abdulla went off to work at the usual time. Siobhán filled the bath and had a long soak, feeling she could never be clean again while at the mercy of the abusive brute she had married.

Feeling disoriented but determined to get away from him, she later left the house, knowing she had to escape from his clutches. She started walking on a journey to anywhere, without caring about her own welfare. She still had some money in her bank account back in Galway but did not want to spend any of it, hoping her life would change miraculously and she could go back there.

She just started walking wherever the road took her. She felt she could never go back to the house. She planned to ring her workplace when she was a safe distance away and make an excuse for not turning up for work that day.

She had been walking for almost an hour into the countryside when a red jeep pulled up beside her and its driver asked her if she wanted a lift. He said he was stopping off at the next town and he could drop her there.

Being in a state of total vulnerability and without questioning this man, Siobhán got in and thanked him. But just as she settled into her seat, the central locking system was engaged and he turned the vehicle around the way she had come.

'Where are you taking me?' she screamed in panic.

He told her that he was a friend of Abdulla, who was worried sick about her.

'Your husband believed that you might be going through a nervous breakdown and he asked me if I could help him to find you. He felt you might have left the house, but knew that you wouldn't have gone too far as you didn't have any money. He told me that he managed the money because you, his wife, are not very good at housekeeping. Why would you want to leave a good man like Abdulla? Doesn't he supply all your needs? Haven't you got a roof over your head? He is such a hard worker. So why would you try and walk away from this good man? As a decent appreciative wife, you need to take care of him, because he is providing good home-cooked food and looking after all your needs.'

He dropped her off at the cottage, where a very angry Abdulla was waiting. He put his arms around Siobhán – ostensibly to show affection in front of his friend – and then offered him some coffee and asked him to stay for a while.

'No, you two have some talking to do,' said Abid.

Siobhán knew that twisted look that had suddenly appeared on Abdulla's face and willed with all her might that this stranger might stay on, hoping that he would protect her from further violence. As Abid was making his way out of the door, he turned around and said that he was glad to be able to help the two of them.

'I was glad I was there to help. Now I wish you both well.' He waved goodbye and drove off immediately.

'It was lucky that I came home at lunchtime. I called into the hotel to find you hadn't shown up for work today. Because you're working only part-time, you have too much time on your own – too much time to think.'

He felt she might try to escape again, so he planned to make other arrangements.

'God knows what would have happened to you if I hadn't come home at the time I did today. How could you have tried to run away from me like that? I'm sure there's something wrong with you Siobhán! Who knows where you would have ended up. You need minding … to save you from yourself.'

After that incident, Abdulla decided he would have to spend more time watching her – that was unless he could get a cousin to stay in the house to do the job for him.

Consumed with anger, Abdulla again assaulted his wife after Abid left. He had lost all feelings of empathy and respect for her, and was now consumed by his wish to control her. All she meant to him was easy access to an Irish passport. The fact that she was going to have his baby would cement his selfish aims. But if she miscarried, and the baby was a boy, she would have hell to pay. If the child was a girl then he planned to abandon her, because having a son was paramount to his twisted view on life. That was partly influenced by his cultural background, but also rooted in the cruelty and controlling behaviour he had witnessed and absorbed from his father. His cruel behaviour was heightened by the fact that he was controlling a woman from a culture that he saw as decadent compared to the one he had left.

Siobhán had little sleep that night. Abdulla did not go to work the next morning, explaining to his cousins in work that his wife was unwell.

He pushed Siobhán out of bed to make him something to eat, despite the fact that she felt very unwell after the assaults she had already suffered from him.

'We will have a very good day upstairs, Siobhán,' he shouted into her ear, which meant he wanted more sex, despite her weak condition, both physically and mentally. He dragged her back to bed and assaulted her again. He wanted to show her that as her husband this was how it was going to be and he knew he would eventually break her spirit.

He told her many a time to think of all the women he could have had, but no – he had picked her instead. He told her she was lucky to get a fine man like him, a charming individual and a great provider. She should be on her knees thanking Allah but she was just a stupid unappreciative bitch.

'There are many of my kind in every country and we are people who demand respect and we will get it, if women know what's good for them. Like us or not, all your civilisation will be wiped out in time in favour of ours.'

'I have met many people from your country and they are very decent people. You are just pure evil. There are evil people all over the world just like you, Abdulla,' said a tearful Siobhán, who stopped herself from saying any more in case this remark resulted in another physical assault.

Abdulla had sent for his cousin who lived in Cork city with her family. He asked her parents if she could help out for a couple of months, because his wife was pregnant and not very well.

Early next morning a young woman arrived at the house.

'What's keeping you?' roared Abdulla upstairs to his wife when she arrived. 'Can't you see you're keeping my cousin Hannah waiting? Get down here this minute.'

The poor suffering woman dragged herself out of the bedroom and tried to pull herself together. She was in an awful state as she made her way unsteadily down the stairs.

'Hannah's staying here until you have the baby. Do you hear me now? Answer me, you stupid bitch and stop being rude to my cousin.'

Hannah did not blink an eye as she saw the poor state of Siobhán. She had heard all about this Irish woman who was not giving Abdulla the respect that was due to him as her husband. She had seen that sort of situation within her own family because of the behaviour of her brother's English wife.

She sat down and made herself comfortable. Siobhán greeted her as best she could, asking her if she would like some tea.

'What do you mean, tea?' demanded Abdulla. 'Hannah has travelled a long way and wants her breakfast. That's the least you can do for her.'

It took days for Siobhán to get back to any kind of normality. She waited on Hannah all the time, instead of things being the other way around. In fact, she was barely acknowledged as the woman of the house. She had difficulty walking, as the baby was lying on a trapped nerve. She thought of her own kind mother every day, wishing that she would arrive and pull her out of this nightmare.

Her life was so far from normal now but she knew she had to try to keep everything going until she could think of another way to escape, far away from him. She knew he would continue to beat her and abuse her, making her a prisoner in this tiny cottage.

She had a dream one night that she was with J.P. in their flat in London. She could hear him whistling. He always whistled when he was happy – and she was happy too in her dream. She could smell bacon frying in the pan and her brother shouting, 'Are you going to stay in bed all day?'

But she awoke to find Abdulla lying on top of her. It was 5.30 in the morning. He grabbed her and dragged her from the bed.

'You, lazy bitch, what the hell do you think you're doing? Did you forget I start work today at 6.30 a.m.? And there is no breakfast ready! Who do you think you are?'

He told her again and again that he had paid a high price to give her his good name although she was not even one of his own kind, one that his parents would approve of.

'Well,' she protested, 'I would have had your breakfast ready if you had let me out bed in the first place.'

She decided not to argue any further, knowing what was good for her.

He retorted by saying she was not worthy of breathing the same air as he was.

'You will do your duty and do as you are told at all times.'

He told her she was a stupid bitch for walking into his trap by marrying him, but he knew it was lucky for him that she had. She was his ticket to a lovely new life in Ireland, where the pace of life was slower. He would never go back over to England, because he was enjoying the good life here in Ireland now.

But he realised he would never find the likes of her anywhere again. Nor would he have to go back to a harsh existence in his homeland. That was an experience he never wanted to face again. He felt that by having an Irish wife, he had a higher status in society. And this status provided him with more respect in the eyes of his peers.

He found some money Siobhán had put by for a pram and cot and other stuff for the baby and he demanded that he should have it for his own use. She had been trying to save some of her wages and had managed to hide that cash from him. He pulled it roughly out of her trembling hands as Hannah watched and, as usual, said nothing. So that was the end of the matter.

All Hannah did was watch. She never helped with the preparation of food or with any cleaning in the house. Siobhán knew that this girl hardly ever washed herself. She was a lazy dirty person with filthy hands and fingernails. Siobhán was thankful that she had nothing to do with the food in the kitchen, but the other side of that equation was that Hannah expected to be waited on hand and foot. As far as she was concerned, Siobhán's home was like a hotel, with her own private skivvy on hand. The fact that the unfortunate woman was pregnant seemed not to matter in the slightest. She actually told Abdulla that she would be sorry when it all ended and she had to return home. She did not want to go back there because she knew she would be made to go out to find a job. Till then, she was going to enjoy every moment of her stay. The only problem was that she had been told by her cousin that she had to accompany Siobhán to her place of work on the days that she was working and had to hang around till she was finished, to make sure she did not attempt to run away again.

The management did not allow that dirty untidy young girl to loiter around the hotel lobby, because it looked bad in front of the guests. They felt her presence lowered the tone of the hotel, so they explained to Siobhán that she must go back to her house.

Her boss Mr Kinread was in Siobhán's corner and wanted to help her in whatever way he could. She asked him to hold on to some of her wages, as her husband had found some other money at home that she had saved up for her baby and had taken it for his own use.

CHAPTER 13

The truth begins to emerge

Mr Kinread, the head chef in Mackey's Hotel, always made sure that Siobhán had enough good food to eat. He thought she was far too slim for her height, because her clothes seemed to be hanging off her.

Siobhán's colleagues, who knew the truth about her situation, were more than a little concerned about her. They worried on the days she failed to turn up for work – although those were relatively few.

They were relieved when she returned to work, even though she was battered and bruised and trying to hide her injuries. Her facial appearance was improved with makeup that she had hidden from Abdulla. She applied and removed that in the privacy of the hotel's staff toilets.

Despite her limited capacity to work, Mr Kinread did not have the heart to sack her because of her frequent absence – by now he felt a huge responsibility towards this frightened young woman who would not allow him to bring the Gardaí in to investigate her desperate situation.

Julie gave Siobhán a loan of a cot and buggy in an effort to help out a little. Her children were at university by then and their baby things had been lying in the attic for years.

Abdulla felt no shame in accepting such things and thanked Julie with ostentatious charm and appreciation. He welcomed her handouts because as far as he was concerned, that old bitch had plenty of money. If she lived in his country, manners would be put on the likes of her. Siobhán would never let Julie know what Abdulla really thought of her and her husband.

After yet another violent blow-up, Siobhán was afraid to go to bed, and slept in an armchair by the fireplace. In that vulnerable situation, Abdulla saw his chance to really teach her a lesson. He wanted her to know without any doubt that her life belonged to him and to him only, and he wanted her to realise that once and for all. He was sick of trying to get that fact into her thick head as he saw it. He took a pair of scissors while she was sleeping and quickly cut off her long blonde hair, so that those men where she worked would not look at her or admire her in any way. By right, she should not have been working at her stage of pregnancy he thought, but this was his new country and he accepted that they had different employment laws in Ireland.

Siobhán spent a while trying to fix her short hair as tears streamed down her lovely face after Abdulla had gone to work. She looked into the mirror and was shocked to see a stranger staring back at her – a woman she did not know with hollow cheeks, broken teeth and now without her lovely long hair. She was deeply shocked at her appearance, all brought about by the criminal behaviour of her so-called husband.

She made her way to work in a pitiful state that day. She never told anybody just how badly her husband was treating her, but her boss took a look at her the minute she walked through the kitchen door, with her red puffy eyes exhausted from crying, and asked who had cut her hair and abused her like that. He held the phone in his hand and was about to call the Garda but Siobhán pleaded with him not to do so. She felt that a Garda investigation might drive Abdulla to further lengths and make her life even more unbearable. She made that decision even though she knew that everybody must have been able to see the truth about what was going on in her domestic life. After all, her face and general appearance told their own story. Not for the first time, Siobhán wondered when her self-respect had deserted her, and why was she was still living with this dangerous individual.

Mr Kinread was kind to this troubled young member of his staff and told her a few times that he was very worried about her. He asked her what she wanted to do about the whole situation, telling her that the choice must be hers.

He made an appointment with his dentist for her because her husband had broken one of her teeth and it needed urgent attention. He also paid the dentist's fees. Siobhán felt such gratitude towards this decent man but she also felt she was a hopeless case, wondering why she continued to live with a brute like Abdulla. Had she lost self-respect, and where had her dignity gone?

Hannah walked everywhere with Siobhán and hardly ever spoke a word to her. It was such a bizarre situation for her to be in. She always worried and was on her guard when Hannah was around. She never spoke to Julie in front of her, afraid that Hannah could understand everything that was being said and would repeat it all back to Abdulla.

'Only a sadistic mean bastard would leave a vulnerable and pregnant woman in such a state,' said Mr Kinread to his colleagues in the kitchen. 'I have never seen a person go downhill so fast. When Siobhán started working here she was an elegant, self-assured woman. But look at her sad demeanour now.'

Ireland was a free country, yet this pitiful woman was not able to walk away from this sadist and return to her good family. How could such a thing happen in this day and age?

CHAPTER 14

Little Fatima arrives

The time had come at last for Siobhán to have her baby. Abdulla refused to drive her into the local maternity hospital because he was on the way to work. The place where he worked had a large delivery of meat arriving and he was the only one with keys to accept the delivery at that hour of the morning. As far as his wife was concerned, she could do as she liked. His work took precedence over the birth of his own child.

Siobhán knocked on Julie's door at five o'clock that morning. She hated herself for having to ask for help, and for feeling so vulnerable, but she had to use Julie's phone to ring for a taxi. She explained very apologetically to Julie that her waters had broken and that the time for the birth was imminent, but that Abdulla had to go to work.

'Well Siobhán, that was very selfish of your husband. He is utterly irresponsible to expect you to cope yourself at this most vulnerable time.' She said this with a note of extreme shock and annoyance in her voice.

'You don't understand,' said Siobhán, trying to justify the actions of her monster of a husband. 'There was nobody else to open up his workplace.'

She was shaken and confused, with a tinge of fear at the thought of giving birth. Almost whispering and standing back, she again offered her most sincere apologies for disturbing her landlady so early.

'Hold on a minute while I slip on my clothes and get my coat,' said Julie calmly, looking very concerned at the plight of the poor frightened soul standing at her door. 'Get your bag and when you are ready I will bring the jeep from the garage. Do you need a cup of tea before we leave?'

Siobhán said she felt sick even at the thought of eating or drinking anything just then and thanked her profusely.

Julie, calm and in control, drove the fearful expectant mother to the hospital and stayed with her for the best part of the morning.

A member of the hospital staff finally located Abdulla by phone and summoned him to the hospital. Siobhán did not want Julie to go but knew that she had to get back to her busy life.

Now Siobhan felt she was being left at the mercy of a monster. Her husband arrived grudgingly but immediately made his way out the back of the hospital to smoke a cigarette. That was the last Siobhán saw of the father of her child until the nurses went looking for him a couple of hours later at the request of his worried wife.

'Congratulations on the birth of your beautiful little girl,' said the midwife when Siobhan finally reached the end of the ordeal of giving birth alone in the company of the very experienced maternity nurses. 'A May baby! A beautiful daughter for you both.'

Abdulla was certainly not a happy father and stormed out in a rage. It was plain to see how unimportant this little girl was to her father. The young nurse was astonished by his actions, as he displayed an unbelievable level of insensitivity on a day that would have been one of great joy for a normal parent. He had wanted a son and he vowed Siobhán and their daughter would pay a high price. He mumbled to himself as he raged through the hospital corridors.

Siobhán was brought into a bright ward with cream and yellow curtains that made the room look very fresh in the early afternoon sunlight.

'God, it's lovely in here,' she said to nurse Mulligan, looking at the name tag on her uniform. For a short while, she felt calm and cared for by the team of cheerful nurses and never wanted to leave the safety of that room to go back to the dark house she shared with the evil man who masqueraded as her husband.

Before Siobhán left the hospital, she spoke to one of the kindly doctors and explained how bad her life was at home and asked if it would be possible for him to give her something without her husband knowing that would prevent her getting pregnant again straight away.

This doctor knew some of her history and agreed to help her. He prescribed her the contraceptive pill as a cycle regulator but explained that if her situation wasn't so serious he wouldn't have given her the prescription, as he was not supposed to make such a service available unless it was a matter of life and death.

The first thing Abdulla did when the baby arrived home from hospital was to shave the child's head and he continued to do so, much to Siobhán's distress.

He would leave the baby in soiled wet nappies for hours on end when he was around, but he made sure the child was dressed well when the nurse came calling to check her development.

When the nurse asked why the child's bottom was raw and sore, he blamed his wife, saying she was lazy and refused to change the child when she wet her nappy – something that upset and hurt Siobhán very deeply.

Abdulla was always on his best behaviour if he happened to be home when the nurse was around, so whatever Siobhán told her about his usual dreadful behaviour, she would appear to be a liar. Abdulla needed to punish Siobhán for giving him a girl when she knew how much he wanted a son. So he was going to ensure she got pregnant again without delay and she would bear him his heir this time. When the nurse left, he slapped Siobhán hard across her face, leaving the marks of his fingers imprinted on her soft pale skin. 'That is for not acting like a loving wife in front of the nurse. You won't let me down again. Will you?'

Unfortunately for him, the nurse had deliberately left her briefcase beside the couch as she sensed something was badly amiss between the parents. She ran back into the house just in time to see Siobhán's red face with his finger-marks still on it. She told Siobhán she would make out a report about her husband's outrageous and criminal behaviour, while he ignored her with his back turned to her, pretending he was busy in the kitchen.

When Siobhán tried to go to her daughter's aid, he would not allow her. As a result of this treatment, the poor little child developed a bad scalding rash on her bottom and was in a great deal of pain. But Abdulla did not care at all, well why would he?

'That stupid nurse won't save the two of you, because I will stand up to all my accusers and deny everything. Let that miserable baby of yours stay in pain. I didn't ask for her!' He knew he had no choice now but to put up with her, he said, as he raged at the fearful mother and young child.

'If I had my way, she wouldn't be around at all,' he said. 'She's like a brick around my neck – and nobody, absolutely nobody, is allowed to be that. You little black-haired bitch – you don't even have your mother's colouring. If she had your looks, then she might be more pleasing to the eye,' he said to the child's mother, who could hardly believe that a father would speak that way about a tiny innocent baby. Abdulla was trying to escape his roots and resented his daughter's colouring, being a constant reminder of where he had come from. After all, he felt he was now a man of the world, a man to be respected. Though he would have liked to look more European with blond-highlighted hair, even though he was now older than when he sported that look in London.

Siobhán was at her wit's end trying to protect the little child they had called Fatima, as the child continued to screech in agony. She tried to grab the baby and run as fast as she could away from

Abdulla, but he threatened both of them with a knife he used for cutting off chickens' heads. He told her that people also get decapitated in some countries for not obeying the rules. He then threw her to the floor and assaulted her unmercifully.

The tiny baby's screeching had turned to a whimper. He would not let Siobhán go to her. This was all about punishing the two bitches in his life, one of whom was a burden to him. If only he had a son, there would be no need for either of them. Abdulla had been rolling around an evil idea in his head for a while and thought he just might have something else in mind for the helpless Siobhán and Fatima.

He knew that it was time he phoned his mother and father and asked for their forgiveness about leaving Pakistan and to ask his mother for help in the rearing of her granddaughter.

He knew his mother would not refuse her grandchild and hoped his father would forgive him too. His plan was for his mother to rear the little bitch, back home in Pakistan, and he would see then what he would do with his wife.

The night-time was the worst, because the child was a colicky baby and could not sleep well. She cried all night, leaving both herself and Siobhán exhausted.

Abdulla made them sleep in the small hallway, inside the front door. It was cold, but he closed the kitchen door firmly behind mother and child, warning Siobhán that his sleep was not to be interrupted.

They were fortunate, Siobhán thought, because it was September so not very cold at that stage.

Siobhán was only allowed back into the kitchen to make his breakfast and then sometimes into the bed with him for another twenty minutes to satisfy his pleasure.

The minute he went out the door to work, Siobhán heated up water for a bath and brought the baby into it with her. After a long soak, she dried the child and rubbed cream over her tiny, blistered bottom, dressing her in warm comfortable clothes. After a warm bottle, the child settled down for a few hours. All was calm then, if only for a short time.

Siobhán had got used to Abdulla's nightly routine. It started with him dragging her to bed, then later on kicking her out, before doing the same all over again early each morning. She hid a couple of small blankets and some clothes, along with a wet facecloth, a towel, some nappies and a bottle of milk for the baby and wrapped them up tightly in an old bag.

Fortunately for Siobhán, Abdulla never bothered to look behind the door but she half expected that he knew. When he was in work, she had a reprieve until he arrived home each evening. Then the whole cycle of torment started again.

Abdulla had sent Hannah home a couple of months after the baby was born, much to Siobhán's relief. He believed it would be impossible for Siobhán to try to get away from him along with the little girl. The word 'daughter' still stuck in his throat.

CHAPTER 15

Barbaric behaviour suffered by Siobhán

Abdulla decided it was time to introduce some new people into his household. He had met a few shady characters from outside the county who helped him to run a small profitable business in the local markets on the side. They sold all sorts of stolen merchandise from his workplace and other factories around County Cork. These items were less conspicuous when displayed in the middle of fresh food produce, local handicraft gifts and numerous other items.

The men sold the stolen goods in markets at the weekends, moving around to different locations so they would not be recognised. Abdulla's bosses would not recognise any of the men who ran the weekend stalls, making him feel more secure. On Saturday evenings they divided their takings.

Abdulla took two of the men home and insisted that Siobhán cook for them. When she first set eyes on these two characters she knew by instinct that they were highly dangerous. There was something extremely worrying about them. One was tall and skinny, dressed in a navy suit – but he still looked like a crook. The other was a little shorter and also dressed in a navy suit but he also had a sleazy air about him and looked at her through sly narrowed black eyes. Siobhán wondered if they had got a deal on the suits, which were certainly not expensive-looking in any way. They were more like something sold at a street market and were somehow ill-fitting. Abdulla also wore such suits.

Abdulla gave her little money for food, and even though she was an expert cook, she found it difficult to prepare meals for him and his comrades with the resources available. She worried about whether he would think the food was good enough for the three of them. If he found any fault at all, then she was in for another assault of some kind.

'Well now, my friends,' said Abdulla. 'I am not a greedy man, so each of you can have my woman in turn. After all, she belongs to me and I say who can have sex with her. You, my friends, have earned that privilege because of all the money you've made for me today. So who wants to go first?'

Abdulla suddenly pulled a terrified Siobhán by the arm and dragged her into the bedroom. 'Stop screaming,' he bellowed. 'You will upset the baby and you don't want to do that now, do you?' he sneered.

'No, no Abdulla. I am your wife – what are you doing, for God's sake? I won't let those barbarians near me.'

'Yes, you will,' he said. 'It's a question of looking after these nice friends of mine now, unless you want your child to be sent away to my mother in Pakistan. In that case, you will never see her again. So be a good woman now and give these men what is due to them. They are bringing good money into this house and besides I will stay around to make sure that you are alright, so no more needs to be said.'

Siobhán was desperately trying to process this awful new turn of events but was unable to really grasp the reality of the gang rape that was being proposed by her monster of a husband.

He encouraged one of his friends to get into the bed as he pulled off Siobhán's clothes and shoved her in beside him. Abdulla stood outside the bedroom door and listened, and when he couldn't stand not knowing what was going on any longer, he took off his trousers and got into bed beside them. When his friend had sexually assaulted Siobhán, who was now in total shock, Abdulla jumped in on the act of assaulting his young wife also. The other man came in and stood at the end of the bed waiting to take his turn in assaulting this terrified young woman. And Abdulla held his hand over Siobhán's mouth to mute her screams.

The men raped her again and finally left. Siobhán lay motionless on the bedroom floor, only semi-conscious.

Almost unable to speak, she managed to utter the following words: 'You and those filthy animals who raped me will go to jail for these crimes.'

Abdulla sneered. 'But you are my woman – you belong to me. I can do anything I like with my own property.'

He opened a battered old brown suitcase and pulled out their marriage certificate. 'This is the proof that you are mine. Are you blind as well as stupid, you silly bitch? I can do as I please.'

'You might get away with this sort of crime back where you come from, but not here,' Siobhán managed to say to her husband, although she could not quite take in what had happened, because she was mentally crippled following the rape by these three men, that had included her husband also.

It was getting late in the day when Siobhán crawled onto the mattress, every movement a complete agony for her broken body. She waited until eventually he fell asleep. She then crept to the bathroom to try to scrub away the filth that had attacked her body after her horrific ordeal with those filthy rapists.

Almost without being fully aware of what she was doing, she walked towards the front door before remembering Fatima. Could she make it as far as the Garda station before he woke up? Or could she run to the Herberts' house for help? In total turmoil, she tried to consider her options in her scrambled mind, but Fatima suddenly started to cry. She made her way back to her daughter's cot and then froze with fear as Abdulla started shouting at her to sort out the little bitch, adding that he wished that she never existed and was out of his life for good.

CHAPTER 16

Weekly rapes without boundaries

Siobhán's mother, unaware of the nightmare life her daughter was leading, regularly posted money to the local chemist in Clonakilty for Siobhán's prescriptions and to purchase some sanitary wear. She had no hope of buying these items for herself because she was no longer working at the hotel. She kept them well hidden from Abdulla. As far as he was concerned, she had no money and could not buy any luxuries for herself. In his view, she should be pregnant all the time and it was up to him to make sure she was. Abdulla prided himself on knowing that he was well able to produce children and if he had more daughters, he would send them out to his family in Pakistan.

He planned to keep going until he got his son, who would be kept here in Ireland. Fatima was a thorn in his side, so there would be no luxuries for her. She could have minimal food and her mother could buy her clothes in the second-hand shops.

He made Siobhán account for every penny she spent on groceries. He regularly warned her against even considering leaving him, telling her he had friends everywhere, all on the lookout in his best interests.

Siobhán just could not understand why she failed to get up and go – especially since weekly gang rapes had started a month ago. It was so awful but she could not bring herself to tell anyone that she had basically become a whore. Who would believe her? Abdulla bought sexy underwear for her to wear at the weekends and made her undress in front of the men. He boasted that by allowing them to get into bed with her, he got more work out of them. She was his commodity – pure gold, providing him with the means to invest in a business that would secure his future.

Siobhán was too frightened to make a complaint to the Garda now, though she had tried to get out of the house to alert them when the men first raped her. She was terrified of all the publicity her case would generate and the shame that would bring to her family.

Abdulla threatened that he could make either herself or her daughter disappear. Either way, she would never see her daughter again. So she settled into her weekend routine as an unpaid whore, terrified to displease her monstrous husband. After all, he still boasted that she had a roof over her head and food in her belly and he was providing well for the family. He even tried to convince her that what she was involved in was normal. So she had to do her bit for her husband and stop complaining about his good friends.

'After all, Siobhán, they are selling loads of merchandise to make money for you, me and our daughter.'

But Siobhán knew that all the merchandise was stolen and knew that her husband and his friends were not only rapists, but common crooks.

Abdulla had an air of excitement about him at the weekends and had no qualms about the morality or criminality of what he was organising. There were no rules in his sex games, because all such notions went out the door when he took part with the men in the repeated sexual assault of his young wife.

CHAPTER 17

Serving the needs of Abdulla's friends

Siobhán was feeling totally bereft by the horrible situation she found herself in – a forced prostitute's relationship with three evil men, a world away from the life she had once had and the woman she once was. She still could not fully acknowledge in her head or heart what she had become. She was now giving herself willingly to these men and there was no reason to think that her situation might improve any time soon. Proper sexual relations were meant to be between a man and woman who loved each other, but she was now engaged in totally depraved behaviour.

Her predicament took over everything else in her life and she spent much of her time naked on her back in a rickety old bed. She was exhausted and her body hurt constantly.

The life Siobhán had once known was gone forever, but how could she complain? She had brought this on herself by agreeing to marry a sadist, wife beater and criminal, and this is where she ended up. How could she have known!

Siobhán thought of ringing J.P. for advice but at the same time she did not want him, or her parents, to know just how bad her situation really was. What would they think of her? Abdulla had tricked her into believing he loved her and had coaxed her away from all that she knew. After all, he was her charming friend over in England and at that stage it seemed he would have done anything for her. But now she knew that he only married her for his passport and to control her – his own piece of very important merchandise.

Mondays and Tuesdays were spent preparing the meals for the week ahead and putting them into the freezer. Wednesdays were for cleaning up the cottage. Abdulla would not bring his friends into a dirty house and warned his 'lazy bitch of a wife' to make more of an effort.

On the nights she was 'working', Fatima was put to bed early with a few spoons of drops to put her to sleep. Before his 'friends' came over, Siobhán took a long hot bath with sweet-smelling aroma oils to make herself even more appealing. Abdulla maintained that his sleazy comrades needed something worthwhile as they were making good money and selling a lot more of the stolen merchandise for Abdulla.

During the day, Siobhán had to make sure everything in the cottage was spotlessly clean and Fatima was given toys borrowed from Julie to play with in her playpen. By the time Siobhán was ready to get her child's food, the baby had usually been whimpering for a while, covered in dried rusks all over her skin and hair. Siobhán had to prioritise getting everything ready for the men in her life now, so Fatima's needs were pushed into second place.

On Saturdays and Sundays, Abdulla prepared a bath for his exhausted wife – not that he cared about her at all, but because she was the commodity he was selling and he wanted to ensure he continued to make good money.

Abdulla's friends admired the kinky underwear that Siobhán wore.

Abdulla insisted that Siobhán eat only salads and other light food. She must not put on weight, now that all the baby weight was gone. She could not allow herself to become a pig, a big slob, he told her; this diet, he maintained, was for her own good.

He counted out little white tablets he called vitamins which he received by post from one of his pals over in England. He made her take them daily to give her energy for her 'busy life'. She would be no use to him if she was not able to perform in the bedroom and to serve beautiful dinners to her guests and he knew that excellent food was something she was well capable of turning out.

CHAPTER 18

Abdulla's pals relent

Fatima's presence was becoming a problem for Abdulla and he decided it was time to pack her off to her grandmother. He had to get her out of the way and now was definitely the time. He would send money home for her keep as he knew his parents would demand it, but he figured it would be well worth every penny.

He did not want any emotional complications with mother and child, so the sooner Fatima was sent away the better for everyone's sake. Then he need have nothing more to do with that little black-haired bitch, leaving it up to his mother to do the rearing.

Abdulla accompanied Siobhán to her next doctor's appointment and sat with her while the doctor gave her a thorough examination for the bad headaches she was having. These caused blurred vision at times. The doctor asked how long she had been having these headaches. She told him she wasn't sure although she knew they had started after that first night she was assaulted by the two strangers with her husband's permission. Her doctor decided to give this young frail woman a full check-up.

Abdulla needed his wife in full health if his business was to succeed, but other than that he could not give a damn.

When Abdulla beat her, he said it was for her own good and she half agreed with him. After all, she must have annoyed him unduly and so she begged for his forgiveness.

Doctor O'Brien asked Siobhán why she had so much bruising on her buttocks and her breasts.

'Well,' she told him, 'we are a married couple and my husband likes playing physical games in the marital bed, and, and of course we love each other and we are very happy.' In Abdul's presence, she was trying to tell her doctor with her eyes that everything was not well at all, but she knew he could do nothing at all for her if she was not straight with him.

She looked the doctor straight in the eyes. Abdulla gave his wife a loving kiss but her doctor was not at all convinced by this act and he knew her eyes told another story. He also knew she could not tell him the truth with her husband sitting beside her.

The doctor asked Abdulla to step outside the room for a minute, but he objected, afraid the doctor would get the whole story out of Siobhán.

'Look Mr Hussain, you have no choice in the matter, as I need to do my job properly,' he said as he held the door open for Abdulla.

'Tell me Siobhán, what is really going on in your home life?' Her lower lip began to tremble and she told him that he had to let her husband back in or her life would be hell when she got home.

The doctor relented and agreed to let Abdulla back in after writing out a prescription for the headaches and telling her that if they continued he would send her to an eye specialist. He knew this woman was in danger but he could not do anything about it without her permission.

Abdulla made it clear to his wife that he must stay with her in the doctors' clinic 'for her protection during any future visits'.

'What protection do you mean Abdulla?' she asked him.

'We must all do what is required of us to keep the family going, Siobhán. And now you must understand why it has to be this way,' he replied without answering her question.

It was with a heavy heart that Siobhán nodded her head reluctantly in agreement; she was in fear of losing her daughter if she failed to play his evil games.

The two men who were exploiting her sexually told Abdulla that they had no complaints with Siobhán's performance, saying that she was learning well and was always willing to have sex the way they liked. She moved her body to any position on the commands they gave her and they were delighted with this gem of a woman who could last the night with the three of them. They wondered what Abdulla was doing to give her so much energy.

Finally, when they had finished, Siobhán felt sick to the pit of her stomach and fell into bed for a couple of hours sleep. On Sunday mornings, after her long ordeal the night before, she was back up to make her husband's breakfast to avoid a beating for not listening to him – telling her that she was not paying attention to every word he spoke in front of his workers. She usually paid a price for letting him down.

One Monday morning as he was getting ready for work, he gave her a hard slap across her bottom telling her she was nothing more than a whore now. He pinned her against the cooker and pushed himself against her, pulling up her nightdress.

'When I am finished, you can finish cooking for your man,' he sneered.

Siobhán knew he could assault her for nothing at all so on impulse she turned around, feeling no fear and hit him on the head with the frying-pan.

'Get your hands off me, you brute,' she shouted, not caring if Fatima woke up. Abdulla was stunned for a moment.

'Well now, you will pay for this, you bitch! Surely you know we are making good money so why are you assaulting me?' he roared, as he rubbed his head.

'No, you have it all wrong, you mean bastard!' she shouted at him. 'You are making good money off me, you, filthy scum.'

Nothing changed after that outburst, but Siobhán was glad she had hit him and told him how she felt. But even so, she was too afraid to leave, being particularly fearful for the welfare of her helpless little daughter.

'You silly bitch! The men want you to perform better next weekend, so in the meantime we will need to put in a lot of practice to bring you up to the standard that they demand of you.'

The only thing Abdulla could not do was chain her inside the house, but he had friends everywhere and they would look after Siobhán for him and would not let her out of their sight. She was his commodity after all and what a commodity he had to sell.

But he realised he must be careful now that the bitch had started to fight back. There would be no more distractions in Siobhán's life after Fatima was gone. She would knuckle down and get on with her life, always hoping she would get her daughter back – that was the lie that he would feed her. She would come to like her life in time. Don't all whores like their job? Doesn't it bring in good money for them? Siobhán was lucky to have the right men who would groom her well, thought Abdulla.

The trapped woman felt it was hopeless to try and escape, and sometimes even wondered what she was escaping from. Was her husband not good to her – apart from the odd slap on the face or on her body? It wasn't really that bad. After all, there was any amount of perfumed bubble baths for her before the men arrived for her night's work. Maybe she was silly for upsetting her husband? It seemed Abdulla's warped thinking was beginning to indoctrinate her.

Abdulla meanwhile was delighted with a wife who was now so submissive to him. He knew he had finally broken her. She always did what he asked of her and that was to give the men a good time and do what they demanded – and he meant whatever way they wanted her to perform. That was how each night was spent. It was not just plain sex anymore, because the men had upped the ante.

'She has learned all the tricks we have picked up in brothels on our travels,' the two filthy swine informed Abdulla proudly.

The two knew Abdulla was a ruthless man and they would not trust him as far as they could throw him. Look what he was doing to Siobhán – his own wife. If he was capable of that then he was capable of a lot more. So they decided to save some stolen merchandise for themselves, while being very wary of him. In the meantime, they had no complaints whatsoever about three nights a week in Abdulla's brothel. They looked forward to their nights of bliss with this fine good-looking woman and her curvy body and voluptuous breasts. She was worth every penny they paid. They called the shots in the bedroom and she agreed, no matter what – after all, her husband was getting good money for her and everybody was happy.

Siobhán prayed the situation would eventually improve once Abdulla had made his money off her back. The two men spoke openly to Siobhán eventually, out of some level of conscience, and asked her if she was alright with the whole situation, as she still held back a little from them at times.

Siobhán spoke to them about her fears of losing her daughter and explained that it was the reason she had become a whore in the first place.

One of the men said he would talk to his pal and they would try and go easier with her – but if Abdulla was around, then they would have to be seen to use as much force as possible, as otherwise he would think they were losing interest in her services. But in the meantime, they didn't want him to know they were adopting a more humane approach to her situation.

Siobhán wondered what they meant by 'helping her out'. She hardly ever heard the men call her by her first name and she was sensing a certain amount of remorse coming from them – but not enough to stop them abusing her.

They too were very afraid of Abdulla – afraid that he would get someone else into Siobhán's bed. So they said to each other: 'Let's hope Abdulla needs money for a long time yet,' and in the meantime they would do their best to go easy on this young woman. They knew she was no whore but had been forced into prostitution by this very dangerous bastard of a man.

'How will we ever get our lives back to normal if this were to stop?' said Henry to Jack. It was like a drug and they felt they must get more and more of Siobhán.

'We made her the woman she is, so in a way she belongs to us too. Did you see all the lace underwear Abdulla has bought her? And those long black boots?' All this made her a prized whore.

'This is far better than any brothel we have ever been in,' said Jack. 'And look what tricks we have taught her for Abdulla's use. Isn't he delighted with this new wife we have given him – a woman who is a real whore in the bedroom? Isn't that every man's dream?' Jack continued with a sickening laugh.

'Abdulla should be paying us for giving him this dream of a woman. But she must be on something so as not to get pregnant for such a long time. With the two of us in her life now it would be impossible for her not to get pregnant,' said Henry.

But now they were worried. The men decided to speak to Abdulla about the situation and to ask him about travelling up to Northern Ireland to buy condoms, as they were forbidden to be sold in the Republic of Ireland at the time.

'We will have to use condoms if she is to continue to make money and keep everyone happy,' they told him.

The amount of money he would lose if Siobhán became pregnant had dawned on Abdulla. He had been too preoccupied with making money and had totally forgotten that she could become pregnant. A son could wait for now. All Abdulla could think of at that moment was the loss of revenue if Siobhán became pregnant. He agreed they would have to get a supply of condoms. So who could travel to buy them? Jack and Henry said they would both go and bring back what they could. The men made the trip up to the north and brought back a large supply. This arrangement would keep everyone happy, thought Abdulla.

CHAPTER 19

Abdulla considers his evil plans

Abdulla forced Siobhán to write to her parents and J.P., telling them not to worry about her or the child, that she was with a good man who provided well for her, and despite early misunderstandings between them, life could not be better. Abdulla stood over her, dictating the letter as she wrote it. He dropped the letter in a post-box and made sure her family would not suspect anything. Fatima would be the next to go, thought Abdulla, but that matter needed much thought and careful planning.

Within a week, J.P. wrote back to his sister, asking if everything was indeed alright. After reading her letter he sensed that all was not well with her. He asked her to please write to him again, to confirm if his feeling was right or wrong.

Siobhán's parents rang Julie, asking if they could speak to Siobhán, or if that was not possible, they asked if she would tell their daughter that they were worried about her and Fatima. Julie knocked on Siobhán's door but got no answer. She told them that Siobhán was most probably in town doing shopping, telling the worried parents that Siobhán seemed well when she last saw her.

Siobhán was considering how she could escape with her daughter. But she was confused and no matter how hard she tried to think, what was in her head just did not make sense. It was like she could not string any kind of coherent thoughts together. Her life just moved aimlessly from one day into the next. She got dressed up for her nocturnal orgies and got on with it. She knew that she had to tell her family about her situation at some stage. She cried out in anguish to her mother when she was on her own sometimes. She tried to look on this depraved behaviour as her job, her way to earn money for her family and tried not to feel any guilt at all ...

Abdulla's plan was that Siobhán would work as long as she could as his prostitute, so having more children was totally out of the question for now. He realised it would be hard to instruct another girl, who might not reach the required professional standard for quite some time and could also expose his immoral criminal behaviour. By this stage, Siobhán was a top-class whore and hard to match. But Abdulla knew the time would come when she would start to lose her looks and would not be as attractive to her clients anymore. That would mean a serious drop in earnings for him. She was good for nothing else now, but what did he care? He also knew she would never be able to prove anything about her 'work' at that stage if there was an investigation. In his perverted way, he felt she must like her job and she was very good at it. He decided he would be rid of her when the time came, but not for a very long time yet as there was serious money to come in the future from her.

CHAPTER 20

Meanwhile, life continues as usual in London

After Trudy and Amahil had been dating for over a year, she brought him home to meet her parents in Scotland. They liked him from the minute he walked through the door holding their daughter's hand. They felt as if they knew him well already because of the letters they had received from their daughter filling them in on how Amahil treated her so well in London.

Her parents gave them both their blessing to marry when they were ready; they didn't approve of couples living together before marriage – it might be old fashioned values they held, but as far as they were concerned there was no other way.

Amahil wrote to his family back home and asked if they approved of his choice of potential wife. He told them that Trudy was a woman of substance, a frugal and wise person. He told them he loved her and had been made very welcome by her family in Scotland. He received a letter back within the month, telling him that they trusted his judgement and if this girl made him happy then they were glad for both of them and hoped they would be able to come for a visit to London to meet their future daughter-in-law at some stage in the future.

J.P. was fond of the couple and was delighted at how well Amahil spoke about Trudy and how thoughtfully he behaved in her company. He could see a look of genuine happiness in his eyes when he was around her and knew that this young girl was in safe hands.

Trudy asked J.P. for Siobhán's address because she wanted to get in touch with her old friend who had always fought her corner at their workplace; she wanted to fill her in on all the latest London news.

CHAPTER 21

Siobhán escapes to her parents

It was late May, just a couple of weeks after Fatima's third birthday, when Siobhán noticed something different in Abdulla's manner, but she could not quite put her finger on what it was.

He still planned to send Fatima home to his mother, so that he would be free to pimp Siobhán out for most of the week and make a lot more money from her prostitution. He would have sent the child over to his parents a year ago only his mother Abeer was recovering from an operation and was not able to mind a toddler at that time. But now all was back to normal and she would be delighted to have Fatima – her only granddaughter – come to live with the family. Even the child's angry grandfather was in agreement.

Siobhán waited until Abdulla had gone to work and then she began searching the house. She was not sure what she was looking for but suspected he was hiding something. Maybe it was all the money she had earned for him? But somehow she felt there was something more sinister afoot.

An old wooden table on which Abdulla always left his keys stood in the corner of their bedroom. It was top heavy with narrow legs. Siobhán studied it for a while feeling it looked odd, before turning it upside down. There was a strange-looking slit on the underside – like a false top had been fixed on.

She pushed a knife through the slit and it came out the other side. A new passport with Fatima's name and photo in it also dropped out, along with banknotes. There were a lot of notes, which she counted with trembling hands, afraid he would come back and catch her. There was at least £500, if not more, so he must have been holding on to this for his immediate use.

She thought for a moment and suddenly felt ill. She had felt Abdulla was planning something evil concerning her daughter Fatima for some time. And now she knew what it was.

She ran over to Julie's house, falling on the gravel a couple of times before she reached the door and pressed the doorbell with all her might. She waited for what seemed like an eternity, but eventually Julie answered the door and was shocked to see Siobhán in such a terrible state. She asked Julie if she could ring her parents.

After Siobhán had told her distraught mother about her sorry plight, Julie asked her in more detail about what had happened. Siobhán told her about her evil husband's plans for their daughter. Over a cup of tea, Julie helped her to calm down and talk about the attempt to send the little girl to Pakistan against her mother's will.

'Did you not know what he was up to? Had you no idea at all?' asked Julie.

She studied Siobhán's face and didn't know whether it was pity or anger she felt for this young mother for being so careless in relation to her daughter's welfare.

'What brought this about?' Julie asked.

Siobhán could never tell Julie the whole story. She told her that he beat her all the time and was cruel to Fatima, but she didn't tell her what she had been put through during the past few years. She didn't want Julie to know what she had become, for fear of losing her respect. Abdulla had always arranged for the men to come down the back field and in through the back door so no one would see them and the Herberts would therefore never suspect anything was amiss.

Julie asked Siobhán why she had stayed in such a toxic situation.

'Did you not fear for your child before now?' she asked in a shocked voice. 'Fatima should have been brought out of harm's way the minute you suspected that he might be up to something. You told me he threatened to send her away a couple of times, so I don't understand why you didn't go back home to Galway with your daughter.'

Siobhán explained that he had friends everywhere who were watching her every move. She said she was afraid of him as he had threatened her many a time that either she or the child would disappear from these shores if she ever went against him. Siobhán also told Julie that she had relatives working in the Garda Special Branch in Dublin Castle.

During the call to her mother telling her about the planned abduction of the child and her planned dash to the train station the following morning, her parents said they would set the wheels in motion with the Garda if she was ready to make the journey home. Some relatives would make sure she was looked after on the train from Cork and she would be met at the train station in Dublin, before travelling on to Galway. Julie advised her to put the passport and money back where she found it and not to let Abdulla know that she suspected anything that evening when he came home.

This was one of her nights off from her whoring activities. Siobhán carried on as usual when Abdulla returned, acting quiet and submissive, not showing any nerves as she prepared his dinner and hoped that Abdulla was not planning to take her daughter away that evening. Abdulla insisted on her dressing up for him alone. With no clients around he knew he would get everything that was due only to him. After all, his wife was very good at her job, and she gave her husband whatever he desired. She was a woman who loved her husband and would obey his every order, he told himself.

Siobhán got a fright when Fatima gave a loud screech and started to howl with pain because she had hurt her finger. She ran to her with a spoon of honey to try to stop her crying and upsetting everything – Fatima loved honey.

She felt her heart leap with the knowledge that this would be her last night with this beastly criminal – just one more night to feel the wrath of this madman. The nightmare would finally be over, and she and Fatima could finally escape his clutches.

But it was a long night for Siobhán. Abdulla slapped her hard on her buttocks, blaming her for keeping him up when he had work in another two hours. Siobhán fell out of bed from sheer exhaustion, but her husband pulled her back in for another half hour to get the last out of his poor exploited woman. Then he shouted for his breakfast to be cooked.

Siobhán went to the fridge in front of Abdulla and asked what he would like for his dinner that evening. She held out some fish for his approval. She was determined that he would not suspect anything before he left for work.

As usual, Abdulla went to work at 6.30 a.m. Siobhán waited for his van to disappear up the driveway and then quickly made her way over to Julie.

Mother and daughter were facing a long and hazardous journey to Dublin, and then on to Galway. Siobhán had secured the passport and taken all the money and any other photos of the child.

They loaded up Julie's car with Siobhán's and Fatima's clothes, then Julie drove them to Kent Station in Cork city. It was an anxious ten-minute wait for the train, with each passing minute feeling like a lifetime.

Julie hugged the scared young mother that she had come to care so much about, shedding a tear in farewell. Julie gave her a flask of tea and some biscuits and milk for Fatima. From the platform, Julie watched them sitting in their carriage until the train finally departed.

CHAPTER 22

Abdulla's evil pals arrested

Sometimes Abdulla arrived home by surprise during the morning. That morning he was there at 10.30 a.m. He wanted to impress upon Siobhán that there was no escape from him and that he was always in control of her life at all times of the day. The minute he opened the door he knew that something wasn't right. Finding the house empty, he ran upstairs to the table to check that the passport and money were there, only to realise they had disappeared.

Julie glanced out of her kitchen window across the yard over to the cottage. She saw Abdulla run from the cottage like a madman and then drive his van away at breakneck speed, missing young Gwen – the housekeeper's daughter – by inches. She was under the archway playing with her dog. She was uninjured, but unfortunately, the young Jack Russell terrier couldn't get out of the way quickly enough and suffered a fractured leg. Julie and the child's mother ran to the shocked young girl and brought her and the injured animal into the house.

The child was only seven years old and completely hysterical. Julie calmed her down and gave her some lemonade and biscuits, while telephoning the nearest vet to come and look at the poor dog's leg. She made some tea for her housekeeper and herself and talked about how the incident had been caused by her tenant.

Siobhán had told Julie at the train station that she had forgotten her chef's knives that were worth £300, explaining that she would need them if she took up a new job in Galway.

'Do you think that you could get someone to take them down

from the attic for me? I would be very grateful if you could send them to Galway and my father will refund the postage costs.'

She had hidden them carefully from Abdulla – afraid of what he would do with them in a raging fit.

'I am so sorry to ask you Julie, but if you can, it would be a great help,' she said gratefully.

Simon, Julie's youngest son, was home for a couple of days and offered to get the knives. They were taking a big chance and hoped that Abdulla would not come home and find him.

But Abdulla arrived back at the cottage within a short time and Simon, who was six-foot-four-inches tall, had to hide in the tiny attic for an hour. It seemed forever, and he tried not to knock anything over or make a noise. The attic was so small he could not even turn around. All hell would have broken loose if he had been caught.

Julie was frantic with worry for her son and walked around the house trying to keep calm. Finally, she went out into the garden with her garden tools, pretending to examine the shrubs and do some work on her plants. When she could bear it no longer, she went back into the house and was about to phone the Garda when Abdulla finally came out.

Simon waited until he was sure he heard the van pull out of the yard. He then climbed down from the attic and hurried over to his worried mother with the set of knives tightly under his arm, wrapped in a blanket.

Meanwhile, at the train's fifth stop before Dublin, two men dressed in grey suits got on and walked through the carriages. When they came to where Siobhán was sitting with Fatima, they moved a couple of people out of their seats, showing the annoyed passengers a badge of some type and moving them further down the train.

For a moment, Siobhán forgot her worries and wondered what was going on. Were they here to help her? But how? she asked herself. Surely they couldn't have got word so fast and made it down this far from Dublin? Siobhán had not expected to meet anyone on the Cork train or before boarding the train from Dublin to Galway.

They sat down opposite her but did not make contact and did not identify themselves to her. She looked across at them, wondering again who they were and why they were showing their badges to strangers. Surely they must be plain clothes detectives?

She poured some tea and opened the biscuits that Julie had packed for the two of them. Little Fatima clapped her hands with delight when she saw them. When Siobhán thought of how kind Julie had been to her she cried to herself. The two men (who actually knew all about her plight) looked over at her and wondered how she had got herself tied up with a madman like Abdulla.

Abdulla had guessed that the train would be Siobhán's chosen escape route and arranged for his friends to board it at the nearest stop to them. He thought it would be an easy task to get her and the little girl back into his clutches again. All they had to do was abduct them and force them back to their home in Cork. He reckoned they could continue on as a married couple, with him getting everything he believed he was entitled to. Only this time he would not go back to work for a while – instead he would stay around and watch her every move.

Two of Abdulla's friends boarded the train at the third stop before Dublin. They made their way through the carriages looking for Siobhán and Fatima. When they found them, Siobhán recognised her husband's friends and froze in terror. Try as she might, she could not cry out for help. The words just would not come out of her mouth. She looked over at the two men in suits opposite her, thinking all this must be a bad dream.

One of the men stood up and put his arm protectively in front of her and her daughter, revealing a weapon hidden discreetly inside his jacket. Abdulla's pals backed away, but were arrested shortly afterwards for trying to abduct mother and child.

At the next stop, the Special Branch men arranged for local Gardaí to take the two abductors into custody. The two men then accompanied Siobhán and Fatima on the final part of their journey home to Galway.

Siobhán's mother rang Julie to thank her for everything, because without her help Siobhán's escape would never have been possible. The next day, a large bunch of yellow roses was delivered to Julie, followed by a postal order to pay for sending Siobhán's knives back up to her.

Julie and Simon were proud to have played a key role in ensuring the safe passage of the two to Siobhan's family home in Galway and to finally get them away from the evil clutches of the criminal beast who had made their lives such a misery.

Julie and her husband gave Abdulla two weeks' notice to leave the house and then the locks were changed after he departed, just in case he decided to return.

Back in Galway, Siobhán began to piece her life back together in the loving care of her family, away from the horrible ordeal she had suffered under the brute who had dominated her life for years. This took a huge amount of courage and adjustment from an emotional, physical and psychological point of view. She was now free to try to live like a normal young mother with her daughter in the safe and secure world she had known years before.

CHAPTER 23

Pádraig comes back on the scene

Siobhán's family were constantly on alert because the peace they had once known was now gone forever. Even once Fatima had grown to be a young woman, she could still be kidnapped and taken to her father's homeland, Pakistan.

Siobhán worried for her own and Fatima's safety, though she knew they were safe in her family home, but she also realised she must always keep her guard up.

She knew that her ex-husband was capable of anything – a man never to be trusted, a pure evil person she would always be afraid of.

Siobhán went through months of treatment to cleanse her system of the drugs Abdulla had fed her, and many times she felt she wanted to die. He used to stand over her making sure she swallowed tablets, drugs that gave her the endless energy to keep his prostitution business going. It took a while for the drugs to leave her system and for her to regain her normal energy levels.

Siobhán's father organised driving lessons for his daughter four months after she came home. When she had passed her driving test, he bought her a second-hand yellow Mini Cooper the colour of sunshine which lifted her spirits, a new chapter in her life.

She tried desperately to put the horrors of her past behind her. Every time she thought back to what she had become in Cork, she trembled at the thought of what could have happened to her daughter – knowing that there had been a chance of never seeing her again.

Siobhán's parents could not do enough for her and their grandchild. If only they had accepted Pádraig as Siobhán's choice in the first place. Now they were all living with the awful consequences of their earlier misguided actions.

Eight months after Siobhán arrived back home in Galway, Pádraig phoned her and asked if she had settled back into life in Galway. He had heard from her friend Marie that she had come home again. He waited for the right time to ring her, planning to gauge how she was and to see if she still had any feelings towards him. They chatted about life in general since they had last met and Siobhán established that he had no woman in his life. During their conversation she was selective in the information she volunteered, knowing that it would be entirely wrong to tell him all about how life had been during her marriage to Abdulla.

Slowly Pádraig came back into Siobhán's life. He had been ashamed of himself for the way he had treated her years before, when none of the problems that he had created were her fault. He realised it was his own insecurities that had led him to take such drastic action in terminating their engagement. He was more than sorry for the way things had turned out. He had of course been deeply hurt by her father's judgemental comments about him, filling him with an anger that persisted for a long time after she had departed from Galway. He had always loved her and wondered if, despite all that had happened in the intervening years, she still any feelings left for him. Or was he definitely part of her past now? So they had much to discuss as they tried to mend bridges and find a new way forward together.

CHAPTER 24

Siobhán drops her guard

It took a long time for Siobhán's body and mind to heal and for her to look and feel normal again. Psychologically she had been severely damaged from her time with Abdulla. Sometimes she felt her body was disgusting and her mind was filled with dark thoughts. At other times, in a strange way, she even felt she should return to the immoral and perverted life she had become part of. She felt deeply shocked for giving serious consideration to the idea of ever going back to her crazed perverted husband and his criminal friends.

Siobhán would never let Pádraig or her family know that her husband had been her pimp as she worked as his prostitute. She could not put that heavy burden on them. She just had to try to forget everything that had happened to her with Abdulla, so that she could act like a normal human being again – like the young woman she used to be – if she was to have any chance of making a new life with Pádraig. He must never suspect her past or he would surely have nothing to do with her used and abused body. She could never blame him for rejecting her if he found out her whole story.

After Siobhán returned to Galway, her former husband managed to find a family lawyer who organised supervised access visits to their daughter Fatima. It was certainly not out of love for the little girl, but a cynical and perverted way for him to have contact with Siobhán, whom he still saw as his legitimate wife and property. So she had to go through the ordeal of coming face-to-face with this monstrous and scheming criminal all over again.

On one of these visits Siobhán very unwisely met him on her own, based on his excuse of discussing his daughter's education and providing extra funding for her. She felt she was able to handle the situation now that she had gained confidence from being out of his clutches for some time. He pleaded with her to return to him, a request which of course she immediately rejected. Even more unwisely, she agreed to have a drink with him in his hotel room, where he slipped a drug into her drink. After a couple of sips from the glass, Siobhan knew something wasn't right as she felt a heaviness in her body and could not move. Abdulla forced himself on her forcing her to have sex with him.

He tore off her clothes and returned to the beast who had caused her so much pain in Cork. He felt quite justified in having sex with her as his wife and did not see his actions as being the brutal rape of a woman who was so desperately trying to rebuild her life after suffering at his hands for years.

Strangely, she almost enjoyed the experience. Was this an addiction to rough sex, she asked herself? Had her previous brainwashing made her somehow want to revert to form with this brute of a man? And what were these emotions saying about her? Where was her shame and dignity?

She fought these revolting thoughts by knowing she had chosen the chance to bring Pádraig back into her life for the sake of her daughter and her sanity. She would settle for a calm life with Pádraig and only hoped that God could forgive her for considering taking perverted pleasure from having sex with Abdulla.

CHAPTER 25

Siobhán makes a decision

Some weeks later, Siobhán began to be violently ill, which worried her mother greatly. An appointment was made with the local GP, Dr Ryan, at her mother's insistence. The doctor examined her fully and then carried out a test, which showed without doubt that she was pregnant. In fact, it established that she was eight weeks pregnant.

'No! This cannot be happening to me,' said a deeply distressed Siobhán.

'What do you mean?' asked her doctor. 'Is this a problem, Siobhán?' He asked if Pádraig was the child's father, expecting to have things sorted out without too much difficulty.

'No,' Siobhán said. 'I wish he was, but we haven't been in a sexual relationship. No, it was my ex-husband. He slipped a drug into my drink when we were discussing my daughter's future and forced me to have sex with him.'

'Well,' said her doctor, 'what are you going to do Siobhán? Surely you're not thinking of getting back with him? Why did you not report the rape?'

'No doctor,' she said, 'I never want to have anything to do with that man again.'

He handed her a prescription for morning sickness and asked her to come back in a fortnight to see him again.

She told him she was going to break the awful news to her parents this evening, and that she was going to talk to Pádraig, to see what he thought about the situation.

Dr Ryan had seen a lot of women in his practice throughout his career in such marriages and could never understand why the wives stayed under such horrendous circumstances. He also knew some women could not afford to leave the family home, in most cases with nowhere to go, and with little or no money of their own. He felt Siobhán was lucky at least to have her loving family. At the same time, he was deeply troubled to hear about the forceful action of her ex-husband, whose actions seemed to constitute rape within marriage.

Siobhán sat down to tea with her parents, although she had no appetite to eat anything. Her younger brother Sean was out at his friend's house and Fatima was staying with Siobhán's cousin for the night. Pádraig rang to say he was running a bit late but was on his way. Her mother asked Siobhán how she got on with Dr Ryan, hoping she just had an upset tummy.

Siobhán was feeling sick with nerves, wondering how she was she going to tell them what the real cause of her sickness was. Siobhán got up from the table slowly. She could not feel her feet on the ground – it was as if she was moving in slow motion, just gliding over towards her mother, as her eyes began to fill with tears.

'I'm afraid I have some very upsetting news to tell you.'

'What do you mean?' asked her mother, with a puzzled look on her face, trying not to let the thought of her daughter having cancer enter her head.

'Do you remember when Sean brought Fatima home from the hotel a couple of months ago? I told Sean I needed to talk to Fatima's father? Abdulla asked if I would stay to talk about extra maintenance money to look after Fatima's school expenses. He went on to say how sorry he was about all that had happened and, before I knew it, I was in his hotel bedroom where he gave me a glass of wine. When I drank it, I immediately felt very strange and suddenly he began pulling my clothes off. I tried to stop him, but I was paralysed, unable to move, because he had spiked my drink. I was totally there in my head, but my body failed to function as I wanted it to. What I really wanted to do was to run out of there as fast as I could. He was telling me that I was still his wife and reminding me of when we took our wedding vows. He told me I had said I would stay with him "till death us do part". So he said he was entitled to have sex with me – and that I was still his wife. Now we were back at the beginning and he would not recognise any future divorce.'

Pádraig arrived in the middle of this traumatic revelation in the O'Rourke kitchen. It took a few minutes for it all to sink in.

'Do you mean that he drugged and raped you Siobhán?' asked Pádraig.

'He said that what he did was legal, as we are not divorced. And he told me that I had kept him waiting far too long for his marital rights. Imagine that for warped thinking. When I managed to get away from him, I struggled to walk out of the hotel without falling over because I was still drugged. I got some odd looks from people as I staggered over to the hotel door. But according to Dr Ryan, the result of that encounter is that I am eight weeks pregnant.'

He parents and Pádraig gasped in shock.

'What, you mean to say that having got away from that bastard, he has made you pregnant again?' asked Pádraig, his voice choking with anger and disbelief.

Liam was putting on his coat and making his way over to the door.

'Where are you going?' said Bridget.

'To get the bastard! Even if I have to drive down to Cork, I will get him. I will get a few friends of mine and he will be dead, buried in a bog somewhere, where he'll never be found again.'

'Hold on a minute, Liam. The decision to meet him was Siobhán's entirely,' said Pádraig, looking over at Siobhán. 'Why didn't you report him when this happened?'

'I just wanted to get away as fast as I could. I was thinking of Fatima.'

'What do you mean?'

'Her father being accused of rape. When she is older, how would she handle it? Would she blame me for pressing charges against her father or would she hate him for what happened? I was so confused that I decided just to put it behind me. But now I don't know if that is the right thing to do, knowing that I'm pregnant.'

Pádraig went over to Siobhán and asked her straight out if she wanted to keep the baby.

'No, of course not! How could I?'

She felt so violated, and terribly stupid.

'That's what Abdulla always said about me, that I was a stupid blonde bitch with nothing in my head. But this time he won't win! I never want to see that evil man again.'

Finally, Siobhán looked over at her father with concern. 'Dad, he's not worth it. I wouldn't waste your time on him.'

She told Pádraig she was releasing him from any commitment he had made to her and that she was sorry for the whole mess. She would go over to England and have a termination, because she couldn't have a child that resulted from rape. She would never be able get the foul image of Abdulla out of her head every time she looked at the child.

Both Liam and Bridget stood back with a look of horror on their faces as the seriousness of the situation sank in.

Pádraig put his arm reassuringly around Siobhán. 'Nothing has changed my feelings for you, Siobhán, so whatever you decide, I will stand by you,' he said, much to Siobhan's parents' relief.

Siobhán rang her brother J.P. in London later, filling him in on everything. She asked him if it would be alright if she went to stay with him while she made arrangements for a termination. She knew J.P. would understand. He definitely understood that it was not possible for her to go through with having this child under any circumstances whatsoever. J.P. cursed the bastard that had tricked her into marriage and had made her life such a misery.

'Well if you're sure, Siobhán. If this is your decision, you'll have to go through with it. And if it means that you will never see that pervert again, then I'm sure you're doing the right thing You will still have your daughter, and you won't have to take any more from that sick brute Siobhán.'

CHAPTER 26

Siobhán returns to London

J.P. was standing in the arrivals area at Heathrow Airport, waiting for his sister. He only wished it were under happier circumstances.

It seemed a familiar sight for Siobhán, as she looked around the interior of the airport. Her brother looked at his sister coming through the doors and was overcome with love and pity for her.

Siobhán studied her brother's style. He was no longer the greenhorn that had come to London what seemed like a lifetime ago now. The pair embraced and went to a café in the arrivals area.

Siobhán became emotional as she thought back to those earlier years, thinking about what might have been … if she had not made the terrible mistake of getting married to a pervert. She apologised to J.P. for asking him to become part of her awful situation.

She had the name of the clinic and had made her appointment already. It was situated just off the Holloway Road. The doctor who would take care of her was a recognised expert and she knew she would be in safe hands. But would she have the courage to go through with it? She knew in her head she must do so, but her heart was telling her something else. J.P. encouraged her without any hesitation and told her she was making the right decision.

'You had no choice in the matter when your daughter was born, but you do have a choice in this situation, do you hear me Siobhán?'

She suddenly felt faint and quickly steadied herself, sipping a glass of water.

J.P. repeated that he would support her, no matter what.

She was not on her own to manage this crisis. J.P. had some money put aside for her to help out in this awful situation. He also had some days off work and they would come in very handy now, leaving him to have time to spend with his sister when she needed him so much.

He told her Jim was coming over later and they would have tea out somewhere. Jim was always cheerful, lifting everybody's spirits. He was also very good in difficult situations and would definitely give her some good advice.

'Sure hasn't he seen it all, Siobhán?' he said, squeezing his sister's trembling hand. It felt like when they went to Mass as young children many years before, him being the older big brother looking out for his baby sister and holding her hand.

And now he would have to step into those big shoes once again for his younger sibling. As he spoke those words, J.P. was also thinking about how unfair it was. After everything she had been through, how could God allow this to happen to her? Did she not have enough hardship with all the beatings she had received from that controlling fucker, he thought.

Siobhán was glad he didn't know the half of it. The fact that Abdulla had sold her body was something Siobhán would always keep to herself, well hidden inside her shattered mind. She still couldn't believe that she had made it out of that cruel place alive. Thinking about it made her entire body shake, just like the aftershock of an earthquake, when she realised how easily she could have lost her daughter.

She could never trust the liar she had been married to. When her parents were down in Cork and had urged her to go back with them, he had warned her that she would not see the last of him if she ever tried to leave him. It seemed a long time ago now and he was still her tormentor, but some day she knew she would get him out of her mind completely.

CHAPTER 27

Siobhán has a change of heart

On the day of her termination, Jim arrived early to make breakfast at J.P.'s place.

J.P. knocked on the bathroom door to let Siobhán know that Jim was in the kitchen cooking breakfast, including her favourite pancakes with sugar and lemon. He wanted to know how many she would like.

'He says he's at your service, Siobhán,' J.P. laughed.

But she knew he was also here to give her some moral support. J.P. had brewed tea for her earlier and because the list of instructions from the clinic included fasting, she turned down Jim's kind offer of her favourite breakfast of pancakes. She had three hours before her scheduled appointment at 12.30 p.m.

Siobhán climbed out of the bath and slowly got dressed.

She examined her body in the mirror. She was tall and beautiful still, but even though she knew she looked good, she still could not help looking on her body with disgust. She wondered if it could ever heal after her suffering at the hands of Abdulla. She still felt tied to the brute she had never loved. But she felt her mind would eventually be able to let go of the abuse she had suffered.

'You are an exceptional human being,' she told herself. 'Yes, you've made the biggest mistake of your life, but you've survived it. You've managed to get away from Abdulla, but you came far too close to believing all his lies and promises. You cannot put yourself and your young daughter in such danger ever again. Remember,

Siobhán, you were always basically a good person. You are *not* a whore. That is all behind you now. It's all gone, washed away with the rays of sunshine and the surety of a good future with your loving family. And now Pádraig is back on the scene too and he accepts you as you are.'

Siobhán made her way into the familiar kitchen, full of the smell of Jim's cooking and looked around. She remembered the first day she had arrived in London, full of hope and dreams for a successful future. At that moment, a wave of sadness swept over her, thinking of what might have been.

London had been a truly lovely place to work, and it had been a happy and positive time in her life. But she could not help thinking that if she had not come to London, none of this mess would be happening now.

J.P. watched his sister's distress, grateful that he had been born a male. He would never have to go through what his sister was going through now or have to make such a terrible decision.

Jim gave her a big familiar bear hug, telling her that she was not alone, that she had Jim, and Marreese, and no matter what happened to her, she would always have her London family in her life!

She told them that Pádraig had offered to come with her to London but she felt it was a journey she had to make by herself, as she was going to have to stand before God alone for making the decision to have this termination.

She arrived at the clinic on time and approached the receptionist. She was asked to take a seat and told that the nurse would be with her shortly. She also had to fill out the required forms and was reassured that any questions she might have would be fully answered. Even so, she could not escape feeling a deep sense of anxiety. Despite all the immoral activity she had been sucked into with Abdulla, somehow she felt different about abortion. There was a creeping feeling that it might be a step too far for her. How could she live with this, while her dormant religious beliefs pulled her in a different direction?

She did have a fear of God, but felt such a decision should be made by her and nobody else. This was a lose-lose situation. How could she possibly look at her ex-husband's child, born as a result of a filthy rape and a lot of pain? What were the chances that this unfortunate child would look just like its father?

Life was hard enough with Fatima, the way her little girl had to try to fit in with other children who often taunted her over the colour of her skin. And of course she did not want Abdulla having a further hold on them if she changed her mind and kept the baby – especially if it was a boy.

A small bespectacled red-haired man called Dr Crookhall approached Siobhán, rubbing his hands together as if he was bringing good news. But this was not good news at all, in fact it was a tragedy about to unfold, thought the frightened young woman standing in front of him. Was he always in such good form, she wondered, despite the anguish of all the young women who went through his clinic? It was as if Siobhán was looking at an existence outside herself – an out-of-body experience. She was wondering if she should just start running – but running where and from whom?

'Well now, Miss O'Rourke, are you ready? We must get on with your termination as you agreed. You have made the right choice, considering all your circumstances. I have read your case notes in detail and I believe you have arrived at the right decision. Try to think of this as being like a visit to your dentist. The tooth must be pulled to stop the pain and the same applies here. This is all about making a new start and getting on with your life.'

Siobhán was in shock now, realising that she was in the middle of a very bad storm. How could she put her trust in this doctor? She did not even know why she doubted his professional expertise. He sat down with her, asking in a kindly voice if she was sure she wanted to go through with the termination. He told her that he must ask that question and said it was the policy of the clinic to have the full commitment of each patient, adding that again he felt a termination was best for her.

Siobhán thought hard about it and remembered Padraig's words. She knew the child was half hers. She loved her daughter and in time perhaps she would come to love this baby too?

The nurse called J.P. into the room as his sister was being prepared for her procedure.

'Your sister needs lots of reassurance, maybe you can give it to her?'

J.P. looked her in the eye and asked her, 'Do you want to go ahead with this or don't you Siobhán? Are you beginning to have serious doubts?'

He assured her that he would help her in any way possible but reminded her that she must carry the decision with her for the rest of her life about whether she went through with this termination or not.

Siobhán thought for a moment again and suddenly got down off the trolley and decided to leave the clinic, apologising for wasting everyone's time before she left. She still had to pay the clinic's consultancy fees.

'Don't worry,' said Dr Crookhall. 'This vital decision could only be made by you. But I sincerely hope you are not making a big mistake. May I wish you the best for the future.'

Siobhán was now more troubled than ever.

'How is this going to work out at all?' she asked J.P. He asked her whether Pádraig would definitely support her and what she would do if he did not.

'You know we can always rebook the clinic, Siobhán, if you change your mind. But you know that Abdulla will find out at some stage. You may never get rid of him. He'll continue to cause you pain and worry, of that I'm sure,' said her worried brother.

But despite that blunt warning from her brother, she could not bring herself to go through with the termination of her child.

Now that Siobhán had her decision straight in her head, she could go about making other arrangements for her family – for Fatima, Pádraig and herself. When the time came to have the baby, she hoped her aunt Joan (her father's younger sister) would mind the child once she returned to work as her mum and dad were already caring for Fatima.

Siobhán felt she would be able to work it all out in time and would make sure not to be a burden on Pádraig, she told her brother.

'Well, Siobhán, if this is what you want. You have a very good job with good money coming in. With your qualifications you could work anywhere and earn a good salary,' said her cousin Jim. J.P. nodded his head in agreement, knowing that his sister could stand on her own two feet with some help from their parents.

'Look, Siobhán, you can do anything you set your mind to,' he said.

She rang Pádraig first to see what was really in his heart and if a resumed relationship was possible after all the trauma she had suffered in her life. Could he take on a woman carrying all this baggage and two children that were not his? He reassured her, telling her that if she could handle it, then so could he. This very much set her mind at ease and she began to be more positive in her outlook.

Siobhán returned to Galway to her waiting family who accepted her decision, although they wondered how long they could keep the news from Abdulla.

As the months went on, Siobhán's father and young Sean took Fatima to see her father on his monthly access visits. They never let her out of their sight for the duration of the visit. Abdulla was always immaculately dressed, though he did look odd thought Siobhan's father with his bleached hair against his dark skin. Abdulla was back to being the charmer, an act that he carried off very well, as he tried to disguise his evil nature.

He bought yellow roses for Siobhán and asked Sean if he would give them to her.

Her father rubbed his forehead fiercely, something he did when he was intensely angry. He tried to conceal his anger, knowing that what he really wanted to do was punch this evil hypocrite in the face for making his daughter's life a living hell. He handed the roses back to Abdulla, telling him his daughter would not be interested in receiving such a gift from him and in future not to bring anything for her, because she wanted nothing from him ever again.

'If you want to spend money, then spend it on your daughter,' he said as calmly as possible, trying hard to control his true feelings.

CHAPTER 28

Abdulla's evil plot

As Siobhán reached her eighth month, Abdulla asked Fatima on one of his visits where her grandmother was, as she was never around when he was in Galway. She told him that her mummy was getting a new baby and her nana was with her. Abdulla asked if Siobhán was in hospital, but Fatima told him she did not know where she was getting the new baby!

Abdulla was shocked – now all was lost he thought, with no chance of ever getting her back. But then he started to count the months in his head and came to the conclusion that the child she was carrying must be his, unless it was from the new man in her life. But why would it not be his he asked himself, after that afternoon of pure passion in the hotel bedroom with his beautiful wife? He decided it must definitely be his child.

But then a thought hit him. What if the child was not his? He would then have to let her go, so he would not bother about seeing his daughter anymore.

Abdulla missed having Siobhán as his sex slave. They were good times for him as he saw it and just remembering how good it was made him all the more determined to get her back. But how could he ever do that?

A plan of action was set in motion in his mercenary head. Maybe all was not lost yet? Without saying anything to Siobhán's father, he decided to search the two local hospitals himself, when he calculated the time of the baby's arrival. He found her at the local maternity hospital on the outskirts of Galway, where she was booked in under her maiden name, O'Rourke. As he tried to approach the ward, he saw that Pádraig, Sean and Bridget were taking turns in staying with her. No way was he allowed into the ward, so there was no chance of him getting near her bed to see if the child was his.

But he had to know if the child was his and whether or not it was a boy. The nurse ushered him away from the ward door. If it was another girl, he was not too bothered, but in the meantime he would have to learn to be patient and play the waiting game again. His daughter would tell him everything in time, he thought slyly.

Following the birth of Siobhan's son, the months went by. Pádraig graduated from the Galway Institute of Technology in Architectural Technology during that time, and secured a place in one of the top architectural consultancies in Galway. This was the happiest news ever for both Siobhán and Pádraig.

Siobhán relaxed a bit more with her son, Fatima and Pádraig – at last, life was good. She had decided to give her son her father's second name which was Jonathan, and Pádraig had put his name on the boy's birth certificate as the father, so the child would be known as Jonathan McDonald.

When the child was a year old, Abdulla insisted on seeing Fatima's baby brother to see if the boy was his son. Siobhán had no choice but to admit that he was, as the child looked so like his father and his sister.

Siobhán knew she should have had him brought to court and charged with rape, but who would have believed her?

He would surely spill out her past to save his own neck. And what about her daughter, what would she say when she was older, when she learned that her brother was born out of rape?

Abdulla thought that the bitch deserved a hiding for trying to hold back what was his, and that was not only his son, but her body also. In time, she would know how bad her life was going to get. She had seen nothing yet. She should have gone home with him, the silly bitch. She would pay a high price for trying to hide the boy's parentage and he would see to that.

Abdulla was sure he could still turn the bitch on and make her the whore she was groomed to be – if he could only get her back home. But all that would happen in time, and he could wait. After all, he was a patient man.

CHAPTER 29

An evil plan takes shape

When the time was right, Siobhán asked a local Catholic priest, Father Murt Reynolds, to baptise her two children. Fatima had not been baptised because Abdulla would not allow it. He didn't want the child so why would he put any kind of a blessing on her life was his attitude. Besides, he thought all Christians were infidels, not worth anything. He told Siobhán many times that they should not be allowed to walk in his footsteps.

Fatima's name was changed to Orla Bridget and the boy became Jonathan Pádraig. Abdulla continued to call his daughter Fatima, which confused her. The children were, of course, baptised secretly, without Abdulla knowing about it.

The relationship between Siobhán and Pádraig had blossomed during the interim, and they were now fully committed to a happy future together. They planned a spring wedding in Galway. Siobhan had got her divorce from Abdulla. It was to be a small affair, with only a few close friends attending. They would get a church blessing after they were married in the registry office. The church was small and quaint with *Belleview Church* carved in granite over the door.

Siobhán had kept in touch with her friends Trudy and Amahil in London. Trudy was so excited and glad when Siobhán asked her to be a bridesmaid along with her friend Marie.

Amahil and Trudy had been together a couple of years then. He was a decent gentle human being, and a real gentleman who always treated her very well. As neither of them had been to Ireland, Amahil suggested to Trudy that they make a holiday of it, exploring Connemara and the rugged west coast of Ireland, a place he had been reading about. She readily agreed with that suggestion. Not only that, but, maybe influenced by the forthcoming wedding, Amahil proposed to Trudy, who accepted his formal proposal although she knew that they had an understanding between them already, this would come in time. What a double celebration – Siobhán's wedding and her engagement.

Siobhán wore a long vintage cream lace dress with shoes to match and held a bunch of cream roses in her hand. Her friend Marie was matron of honour and Trudy her bridesmaid. Both were dressed in long plain primrose dresses and carried a small posy of yellow flowers. Siobhán wanted to keep her wedding low-key, without too much fuss. Siobhán and Pádraig spent a long weekend away, a very short honeymoon in Donegal, avoiding the south of the country because of Siobhán's grim memories of County Cork.

The quality of their lives was greatly enhanced as they set up home as a young family. After renting in Galway city for some time, they were finally able to take out a mortgage to buy their own home a short distance out into the countryside. It had three bedrooms, a large, homely kitchen and a comfortable sitting room – nothing too fancy but good enough for their needs. Pádraig had the skills and planned to make any changes that the house needed over time.

Abdulla was still seeking access to his daughter and now his son; he was acting his most charming, even buying clothes for both the children on one occasion. He said it was the least he could do and even appeared to be sorry about everything that had gone on in the past. Now, he claimed, he just wanted to be friends, like they had once been in London.

But Siobhán was not fooled by his cunning behaviour. A shiver ran down her spine when she thought about the dreadful things that followed after her time in London.

She had lived a nightmare and still had trouble trying to get away from those horrible memories.

It was not possible to escape them completely because she saw him occasionally when he had access to the children once a month.

Abdulla rarely missed such visits and always arrived at 1 p.m. sharp. He carried his camera with him just like a tourist, but he had done the same in London, so there was nothing unusual about that. Siobhán told her family that he used to take photos of all kinds of things, especially of Big Ben and other major tourist attractions in London, and would send the photos to friends in Pakistan.

Though Sean was warned to keep his eyes wide open always and watch him closely, they got on with each other, with no tension between them at all. Abdulla treated him like his young brother, allowing him to use his camera to take pictures of things he liked. Abdulla would have his photos developed and give them to him on his next visit, much to 15-year-old Sean's delight.

This went on until Jonathan was three and Orla was eight years old and preparing for her First Holy Communion. Liam, the children's grandfather, would take over from Sean every now and again, and then Pádraig would take a turn. Everyone was satisfied – even Abdulla.

'Sure look, he's like one of us now, he's learned the way Irish people live and has fitted in very well and seems to like us,' said Sean.

'No, he's never to be trusted Sean,' warned Siobhán. 'You must never relax your guard when that man is around. He will always pose a serious threat to this family because he's a source of great evil. Believe me, I know that first-hand.'

But Siobhán did not follow her own advice, eventually relaxing the visiting restrictions a little, almost believing they were out of danger with him at that stage.

She believed that he had been reformed in some way and was getting on with his life as a better and more trustworthy person. Very unwisely, she sometimes allowed him to take the children to the park just down the road unsupervised. These visits have been going on for years so maybe it's time to relax a bit, she thought. One of the family usually kept an eye on him from a distance. This continued for six months without incident, until everyone was feeling more relaxed around Abdulla.

He bought yellow roses sometimes on his visits and would plead with Sean to give them to his sister, just to let her know how sorry he was about everything that had happened in the past. It was the least he could do for her, he insisted, because he still had genuine feelings and respect for the mother of his children.

Sean felt sorry for Abdulla, who had been so stupid in the past. He told his worried mother and father that somehow the man had changed.

Abdulla, meanwhile, was congratulating himself for being so clever, seeing this new level of trust developing into the opportunity he was patiently waiting for. He was leading that stupid bitch into a false sense of security. As he saw it, Siobhán and Pádraig had the responsibility and costs of rearing his children and everything that went with it, including doctors, dentists, schools and so on here in Ireland. He was happy enough about the situation as it was not costing him much money at all. In fact, everybody seemed happy about how things were working out, for the moment at least. But he was playing a dangerous waiting game and would put his plan into action when he decided the time was just right.

Orla arrived home from one of her father's visits and asked her mother if she was a Muslim. Her father had told her that she was and that she should not be making her First Holy Communion and that if she did, she would go straight to hell. Siobhán tried to console her daughter and calm her fears, telling her that it was not true at all and that Father Reynolds would explain it all to her. But the child was afraid to go to bed in case her bed was swallowed up and she was pulled through the floor straight down into hell when she fell asleep. She was afraid that she might die and go straight down into the fires of hell. Her father had told her that she was the devil's child now!

Orla told her young friend Anne in school the following Monday, and the friend ran home after school and told her mother what Orla had said to her. She asked if Orla could still make her communion if she was a Muslim, like her father said she was, and would she burn in hell? The friend's mother rang Siobhán to talk about this very serious fear that had affected not only Orla but her young friends also.

Abdulla had been preparing his move for a long time and felt that the bitch was finally going to get what was coming to her.

'Who the hell does she think she is, treating me like dirt? Imagine calling my son after her father – the infidel. My precious son, my own flesh and blood.'

He pledged that in time, his name would be changed to Arsalan Abdulla, after his own father and himself. The women in his home, meaning his mother and cousins, do not count for very much at all he told himself. They do as they are told by the men of the family and manners have to be taught to them from the time they are born.

Yes, his children were going home where they belonged: his mother and aunt were ready to do the rearing back in Pakistan. In fact, all of his family were waiting for the children to go home.

Finally, they would be integrated into their Muslim heritage. Fatima, his daughter, would take her place with the women of the house and learn what was expected of her. And Arsalan would be his prince, and his sister would wait on him hand and foot. That was how things were done in his homeland he thought in his sinister warped mind.

Abdulla was glad that he had made up with his parents – but only because he needed them to do the rearing of his children. Otherwise, he would have been happy to leave them in his past. He was angry over having to send his children to Pakistan at all, making him beholden to his wretched father.

There were conflicting emotions going on in his head over his parents. He basically cared for them but hated his father and his demanding ways and he knew he could not live their sort of lives in Pakistan.

What he would never admit to himself was that it was really himself he was angry at, for his stupidity and for letting his Irish wife slip through his fingers.

CHAPTER 30

Proving past crimes

Abdulla had warned Siobhán when he raped her in the hotel that no one would believe her if she reported the crime to the Garda. He vowed he would tell them about her previous work as a prostitute back in County Cork. He threatened her with that revelation and assured her that she could not afford for it to get out into the public realm.

She said that was untrue and that he had taken part in the orgies that he organised.

'What do you mean, me taking part, Siobhán? I was your husband, so you were always there for my taking.'

She knew very well that she could not undo what all the men had done to her so, like it or not, that was what she was – a whore – and there was no getting away from it.

So Abdulla was still able to call the shots. He figured she came cheap – a couple of brandies and he could do what he liked with her.

'And maybe you liked it that way – if you are truly honest with yourself.'

Yes, she was still his slave, and he was obliging her by not disclosing that she had been a willing partner to a number of men who paid her for sex. He told her she could have left the prostitute role a lot earlier so why did she stay on? He knew why she stayed. It was because she loved him and no other man could satisfy her in bed the way he could.

But Siobhán had come to realise that Abdulla's threats could not hurt her anymore. She would tell the whole story and that would not look good for her torturer, also realising that emotionally she could never escape from this brute.

So she threatened to report the rape. But did she herself believe that she would never have sex with him again?

Abdulla could not love anyone, only himself. In his twisted mind, he believed the reality was that he controlled her still.

But of course, Siobhán now loved Pádraig who did not have a hateful bone in his body.

It seemed a lifetime ago that all this had happened to her, but the horrendous memories could not be fully erased.

CHAPTER 31

Abduction

'Have the children home in time for dinner at 6.00 p.m. Abdulla. It will give them time to have their baths beforehand,' said Bridget, as she dried her hands in her apron, before giving each of her grandchildren a gentle hug.

'You are not to eat too many sweets now, do you hear me children?' she said gently before they left in an excited mood.

'No problem,' Abdulla said, nodding in agreement. 'We'll have lunch in Supermac's at 2.30 p.m. and just one ice-cream,' he smiled back at the children's grandmother.

Orla was delighted with the idea of not having to eat sandwiches and drink tea out of Mummy's flask that day, but she also knew that her mother would be mad with them if they ate too many chips and burgers, because she always told them that that kind of food was not good for them, being full of salt and fat.

'Well, we'll just have a little treat, children,' said Abdulla, trying to sound as caring and sincere as possible. 'We have to do what your mother and grandmother say.'

They then waved goodbye to Bridget and left, without anybody from the family watching Abdulla's actions; by now, everybody felt more relaxed about him being alone with the children for short periods.

'Wait Abdulla, have you got your camera?' Sean called after him. 'Will you take some photos today?' Abdulla said that he hadn't got it. In fact, the camera was in Sean's room, but he didn't realise that at the time.

Abdulla had plans to get rid of Siobhán's poor stupid brother, whom he regarded as a complete pain. He had become friends with him merely to gain his trust. At times, Sean thought his sister was exaggerating the whole thing about Abdulla being an evil man who needed to be constantly watched, especially when he was visiting the children. He believed he got on very well with him and found him generous to a fault, as he always bought him what he wanted in the shops, and even allowed him to use his camera, later having his pictures developed for him. Being a teenager, he never had much money on him so he found Abdulla to be extremely generous.

Abdulla knew that Sean was putty in his hands, the silly innocent little fool – just like his stupid sister. What Abdulla could never see were honest decent people – a concept he simply failed to understand.

As part of his warped thinking, he reflected on the day he had enjoyed Siobhán's company when he slipped a tranquillizer into her brandy at his hotel. Even if he did force himself on her to have sex, it added more pleasure to have an unwilling participant beneath him. How would anyone else give him such pleasure on demand? He remembered how it was when they were first married, when their marital bed was full of passion, and he was sure that Siobhán remembered also. How could she possibly forget how good things had been?

Sean usually met some of his friends on Saturdays, but Siobhán always asked him to hang around to keep an eye on the children at a safe distance when they were with their father. But that day, Sean felt there was no need to become too involved in such supervision. He was on the way to give Abdulla back the forgotten camera and said goodbye to his friends, making his way down a laneway to meet him. Before he reached the end of the lane, he was attacked from behind by a couple of strange men.

Sean tried to turn around, but fell down, hitting his head on the corner of a rusty skip. He was found later by a shopkeeper who had taken a shortcut up the laneway to the carpark. The young man lay unconscious on the ground. The man cried out for help and someone ran back down the lane to the phone box to call an ambulance.

The shopkeeper searched Sean for some sort of identification but found nothing.

The ambulance took the badly injured young man to hospital, where doctors worked on him for what seemed like a very long time, before transferring him to the Intensive Care Unit.

'Where are we going Daddy?' asked Orla and Jonathan, sensing that something was not quite right.

'We're going on a mystery tour, children. Have you ever been on one?'

Abdulla tried to make his actions sound normal, like it was the sort of thing that children did all the time. After driving for a further couple of hours, they finally reached Dublin Airport, where Abdulla left his car in the short-term carpark for his cousins to collect. All three went inside the building to meet his relatives.

Abdulla had a good head start with the children. His aunt and uncle had arranged everything for him – all the paperwork, including passports for the children – which they showed Abdulla inside the terminal building.

The children were to be passed off as their grandchildren. His aunt took them to the toilet to change from their Western clothes into those of Pakistani children, and pinned name tags onto their clothes with their new names written on the tags – Fatima and Arsalan Hussain. She told the confused and upset children it was in case they got lost. She cut Orla's hair short with a pair of sharp scissors, much to the child's deep distress. She cried out desperately for someone to help her.

'No, no, this must be done. Now, child, behave yourself. You should be happy to be going home to see your daddy's family and to have a lovely holiday.'

Orla cried bitterly for her mother and insisted she was not going anywhere without seeing her.

The poor anxious children were totally confused and frightened and could make no sense of their abduction at the hands of this strange woman who spoke in a strange accent and looked very frightening, forcing them to do things that they could not understand.

In case the authorities were looking for them, they made sure that Orla and Jonathan's appearance and identities had been completely changed.

In order to avoid suspicion, Abdulla had arranged not to be seen anywhere near his children. He planned to take another flight shortly before them, giving the children's guardians a better chance of reaching Pakistan safely.

Abdulla's uncle and aunt arrived at London's Heathrow Airport with the bewildered little children and made their way over to the designated area for boarding a flight to Benazir Bhutto International Airport, Islamabad.

Abdulla planned to catch a flight there one hour before his children, so nobody would suspect anything and to avoid bringing the authorities' attention down on them. He had worked out every move in great detail, and hoped his months of evil planning succeeded without a hitch.

CHAPTER 32

The search begins

Siobhán, Pádraig and the children's grandparents were frantic with worry when Abdulla failed to return with the children at the agreed time that evening. Where had they gone? Had he taken them down to Cork? Bridget and Liam tried to reassure their daughter, telling her not to worry because Sean was with them. But they knew something was not right and they had a hard time convincing themselves, let alone Siobhán and Pádraig.

By 8 p.m. there was still no sign of them, so Pádraig and Liam decided to search the park and the surrounding areas. The family checked with the staff in Supermac's, to see if they had seen the children earlier that day with their father and uncle. The staff examined their photos but shook their heads. They hadn't been in the restaurant at any time during that day.

Siobhán asked her mother to stay in the house, in case the children came back, while she went to the Garda station with Pádraig to report her children missing. She was also becoming concerned for Sean, who had not yet returned home either.

Liam also arrived and the sergeant on duty asked them all to sit down, as they all tried to speak at once.

'Please, one of you at a time.' The sergeant raised his hands to calm the situation down. He looked over at Siobhán. 'Why don't you explain exactly what has happened, from start to finish?'

Siobhán told him the whole story. Her worst nightmare had come true. Abdulla had taken the children and her sixth sense told her that her children were no longer in Ireland.

'We shouldn't be sitting here – we should be doing something to get them back, but where do we start?' she pleaded.

She stood up, not knowing where to turn. 'Why would he do such an awful thing, just when he appeared to be earning everybody's trust? What had he to complain about, when we provided everything for the children and it cost him so little?'

As the sergeant got on with writing down detailed descriptions of the missing children and their father and asking all the relevant questions to get a search operation underway, Siobhán was becoming inconsolable. Pádraig held her close and tried to reassure her as she trembled with shock and fear for her innocent little children who were obviously suffering at the hands of the depraved individual who had done everything possible to make her life a misery before she escaped his evil clutches.

Phelim Murphy, an orderly at the hospital, was sure that he recognised the young man who had just been brought in by ambulance.

'That's Sean O'Rourke I think,' said Phelim. 'He lives not far from me.' He rang a mutual friend who confirmed his identity and the hospital staff passed the details of his assault on to the Garda. It was 10 p.m. and Siobhán, Pádraig and Liam were still at the station when the hospital rang. The sergeant made his way over to the family to bring them the news of the assault and the injuries sustained by young Sean.

CHAPTER 33

Nightmare for the children

Abdulla's aunt and uncle were about to board the long flight for Pakistan with the two very frightened children. They had been warned not to make a scene in front of the air crew and that if they did, they would not be allowed to go home to their mummy in Galway ever again.

The young girl was all over the place with emotion: fear, disbelief and hope that her mother would be able to find to them before the plane took off.

She was too young to grasp the enormity of what was happening to her and her little brother. It was their first time on a plane, so everything was unfamiliar and threatening in her young mind. Should she cry out for help? What would happen to her and Jonathan if she did? Before she knew it, the aeroplane doors were closed and the air hostess was handing out packets of sweets to the children as they settled down on the first part of the long flight to a place they had never been, a place their father called home.

These strange people had forced her to dress in awful clothes that almost covered her whole body and she felt hot and uncomfortable, adding to her misery. She even saw her new 'aunt' stuffing their clothes into a rubbish bin in the Dublin Airport toilets and could not believe what was going on.

Jonathan was hot and clammy and exhausted from crying for his mother, while Orla could no longer hold back her own tears. But they were warned repeatedly about what would happen to the two of them if they continued to cry and attract attention to themselves.

After a very long flight they landed in the heat of Benazir Bhutto International Airport. Abdulla was waiting for them when they arrived inside the airport. He took the children and paid the people who had trafficked them to Pakistan, and then they went their separate ways.

'Where are we going?' asked Orla.

'None of your bloody business!' said Abdulla menacingly.

He now felt justified in ill-treating the poor timid girl, considering that she was now in his country and her life was going to be a lot different – not like it was back in Ireland. Orla started to shiver as she remembered how he had treated her as a very young child.

Both of the children needed to use the toilet and were brought to what seemed at first like the toilets back home, but the cubicles were smaller and not very clean. Orla only used the toilet out of desperation and Jonathan refused to use it at all. They left the airport, Abdulla pulling Jonathan roughly after him. They were both now very tired and frightened, and completely baffled by their experience of this alien place.

'Your names are Arsalan Hussain and Fatima Hussain, do you hear me?' Abdulla growled at the children. When his daughter tried to protest, he hit the child cruelly across her little face. He had waited a long time to sort out this little bitch – to punish her for being born. He had been very good at dishing this sort of punishment out to her mother. All the bad memories from her early childhood came flooding back into Orla's head through her tears and a sense of fear and dread overwhelmed her.

'Oh, mummy and granny,' she whispered silently to herself. 'What is going to happen to us and why is daddy being so horrible and where are we going?'

The bus for Lahore was crowded. There were no seats and hardly any room for standing. Abdulla held on tightly to a screaming

Jonathan, while his sister tried to comfort him. But no amount of attention from Orla could calm him. They finally reached the bus station and then walked for fifteen minutes, Abdulla pulling his son behind him. The child could hardly keep up, his little legs buckling under him, but his father pulled him all the harder, ignoring the child's pain.

The children were hot, thirsty and very tired, but Abdulla made them run almost all the way to his mother's house without showing any mercy towards their distress. He did not care about the long journey they had just made and what they might be going through with no mother around in this alien place, without love and security.

Everyone came out to welcome them home. Abdulla hugged his mother and was overwhelmed with emotions he thought he never had. His father even came out to greet his lost son.

'Well my son, all is forgiven now,' he announced. 'Welcome home and let's start again and leave the past behind us. We both used some harsh words which I am sure neither of us really meant, son. Your mother can get on with the rearing of our grandchildren and we both will keep a special eye on your son, my lovely grandson. Let's have some coffee now and some food.'

'Come here Fatima.' Her grandmother reached out to touch Orla. Finally, she got to meet her granddaughter! 'And look at Arsalan, you big boy! And named after your grandfather. I am so proud of you.' She spoke in broken English that they could not understand. The children took a minute to take in their strange surroundings before they could speak at all.

Their grandmother brought them some food to eat but there were no tables, so they sat on the floor on cushions like everybody else. They tried to eat some of the strange food served to them, but found it very hot and horrible and not to their taste as Irish children.

Very little was actually eaten, with most of the food falling all over the floor. Again, Abdulla treated Orla very badly for slopping her food. After the food was cleared away, aunts, uncles and cousins arrived and gave the confused children presents of new clothes and a school bag each with everything they would need for school inside the bags.

After all the relatives said their goodbyes, they then went back to their own homes, leaving young Orla's head in turmoil.

Abdulla's mother brought the children into their bedroom and opened all the presents. All Orla could see was more awful clothes, like the ones she was forced to wear back in Dublin, before they got on the plane.

'You like?' asked their grandmother Abeer, but Orla sensed something in her tone. It was clear she meant, 'You are going to wear them, like them or not, so whatever you say won't count,' so the child nodded her head in fear and agreement. She did not want her grandmother to tell their father that she was giving trouble or he would surely hit her again. Both children cried themselves to sleep that night, holding on to each other, afraid of what the next day would bring.

Jonathan did not go to the toilet for days on end, and as a result developed encopresis, which left him soiling his underpants and suffering with a sore bottom and legs from wetting himself. His father was at his wit's end as to know what to do so he responded by slapping him for being downright lazy and disobedient towards him and his grandparents.

Abdulla was glad to get the phone call he had been waiting for from Ireland.

'Yes, the job was done successfully,' said Adam Zainab. 'He won't be coming out of hospital for some time – that's if he makes it at all.' He spoke in code, afraid that their conversation would be picked up by the authorities.

Abdulla was beside himself with excitement after pulling off such an impossible task, and could hardly believe he had finally got his children back to Pakistan, away from their mother. Now she had got her just reward, he thought. He was proud that his evil abduction of the two children had gone according to plan. And he didn't care that Sean had been so badly injured – after all, he was just another infidel and the world could do without the likes of him, or so he thought in his merciless little mind.

Abdulla asked his friend if Sean had seen either of them. If he could describe them to the local Garda, if he came around, then they would be in a lot of trouble.

'No, he didn't see either of us. We came up and attacked him from behind, so no, nothing to worry about, Abdulla, my friend.'

CHAPTER 34

Praying for Sean's recovery

Siobhán and her parents made their way to the local hospital, almost afraid of what they might find and not knowing how badly injured Sean was after his brutal attack. A young nurse pointed them towards the Intensive Care Unit, where Sean was on a life support machine. They were not allowed in to see him together, so Liam and Bridget were taken first to his bedside. 'Will he make a full recovery?' asked Liam. He was looking at the hospital staff for answers.

'I just wonder who did this to him– and why? He didn't hang around with a bad lot,' he said, just rambling on, holding his tweed cap tightly in his trembling hands.

'The children are missing,' said Bridget, half speaking to the nurses.

'It must have something to do with Abdulla, it has to,' she said, not allowing her young son's serious condition to fully register in her head.

The nurse shushed them gently.

'Sorry, but this young man has sustained serious head injuries and must have peace and quiet now. We will keep you fully informed of his progress,' she added gently.

Bridget clung to her husband for support, willing him to tell her that everything was going to be alright, but she knew that night that their lives had changed forever, with her young son fighting for his life and her grandchildren both missing.

'I only wish it was a dream,' said her husband, as they made their way out of ICU and over to the waiting area, not knowing what to do next, and feeling totally confused.

Siobhán and Pádraig were talking to a Garda, who introduced himself as Thomas Leonard.

'We're trying to find out what happened to him,' said the Garda. 'He was discovered in a laneway just off High Street. We're talking to a possible witness at the moment, to see if they can shed some light on the situation.'

As they waited for news back at the house, Siobhán was feeling ill. She was worried for her brother and was frantically worried about the whereabouts of her two young children.

'Are they still in Ireland, do you think?' She directed her question at Pádraig , but knew in her heart that she was grasping at straws.

The Garda had told them that there might be some chance if the records of all the airports and seaports were checked out, but so far there were no reported sightings.

They would get feedback within twenty-four hours, when they had checked all the data on flights that had left that day, especially for London Heathrow and Gatwick Airport. The wait was agonising.

When they eventually got a call from the Garda they were afraid to pick up the phone – afraid it might be bad news about Sean, and if not Sean about the children. Siobhán answered, with trembling hands, hardly able to hold the phone, and waited before she spoke, in a mere whisper.

'We have found a couple of children of that age who travelled to London from Dublin by the names of Fatima and Arsalan Hussain, but they were travelling with a foreign man and woman who were their aunt and uncle. Their passports seemed in order and no problem was reported to the authorities. The children would have been probably eight or nine and three or four years old.'

Siobhán was completely shocked, realising that her fears were being realised and that they had probably been abducted. She asked if they had any information on somebody called Abdulla Hussain.

'No, not on that flight, but it seems somebody with that name got a flight over to London Heathrow Airport an hour earlier then these children, and later travelled on a separate flight to Pakistan.'

Immediately, they all knew without any doubt that the children had been kidnapped and taken out of the country by her wretched former husband.

Pádraig tried to console Siobhán, who was broken-hearted over the plight of her children. What were they going to do in this unbelievable situation? It now seemed definite that Abdulla had something to do with Sean being attacked, as he wanted to get him out of the way and buy more time for his getaway the day he took the children. Young Sean had trusted Abdulla, always standing up for him, foolishly thinking of him as a good friend! And now Siobhán's baby brother was lying there lifeless in a coma, fighting for his life.

In desperation, Siobhán pleaded with Pádraig for answers about what to do next, desperately looking for some sort of magical answer to this unbelievable crisis. He had no doubt whatsoever that the children had been kidnapped and taken out of Ireland.

'No, Siobhán, I'm sure now that they are not in Ireland. If he travelled to Pakistan, I'm sure these other two people must have taken the children there too from London. I think it's time we asked your uncle Tim for help. Try and keep calm. We need all of our strength for the job we have to do. Think of it like this, we may be apart from the children for a while but only for a while. Don't worry, we will get them safely home with a lot of help from the authorities. In the meantime, we must pray for the children and for Sean's recovery.'

Pádraig was doing his best to take control of the dreadful situation, while not letting Siobhán see what he really thought about the difficulties of getting the children back, which he could see would develop into a very unpredictable and complex international battle for custody of the little ones.

Over the following twenty-four hours, the family took turns sitting by Sean's bed. When not by his side, the family prayed in the hospital chapel for him, and for the safety of the children. They tried to support one another through the crisis as best they could.

Early the next day, Siobhán rang her father's brother Tim, who had retired from the Garda and was now a private detective. She told him the whole story about the kidnap and the Pakistani man behind it, telling him that they would support any initiatives he could suggest to work towards a favourable outcome.

'You could start by ringing J.P. to find out if he has any clue about who Abdulla's friends are in London. Try to get me as much information as possible. I also need photos of all three of them.'

Back at the hospital, Siobhán poured a cup of tea for her mother and father and sent them to the family room for a short break while she sat with her young brother, feeling she had to take the blame for what had happened him. She should not have left Sean alone to supervise the children and to watch their father, but they were all beginning to trust Abdulla more with the children – who would have thought he would organise a horrific assault like this?

She should never have trusted Abdulla under any circumstances, based on his track record of physical and sexual abuse. She always knew deep down that he was a completely untrustworthy snake. She was indeed the stupid bitch that Abdulla always said she was, she told herself! To think she had got to the stage of trusting him with the children! She knew he was bad news but she never thought he would stoop so low as to have her brother almost killed as part of his evil plan to kidnap the children.

Liam sat beside his son's bed, feeling heartbroken. There was still no sign of movement.

'You have to pull through this son,' he pleaded. He wiped his tears away with a heavy heart. He was also worried sick over his grandchildren and what had become of them.

It was too much for Bridget and himself to cope with.

CHAPTER 35

The children's first day in an alien country

'Get up, children,' Abdulla called out in a loud voice. 'It's time to start school today.' It was 7 a.m. and the two Irish children were about to be sent to a Pakistani school for the first time.

'No, I don't want to go!' screeched Jonathan. 'I want to go home to my mummy!'

'Stop that immediately, unless you want to get punished like your sister Fatima,' said his father.

Abdulla had the back of his hand ready to hit the young child but changed his mind. He had no qualms about giving his son a slap if he failed to show some respect, but first he would try and get around him in a kinder way before he used any kind of force. He felt it would be much easier if the child liked and trusted him.

Orla thought everything in their father's house was dirty and dark. Their home back in Ireland had been nice and clean with lots of light, but in this house the toilets were dirty and she even saw a cockroach that got into her shoe, causing her to scream in fright. The food was awful and she could only eat the bread, which was tasteless and as hard as cardboard. She tried to dress herself as best she could and brushed her short hair. She had no toothbrush because her father told her she had no need for one. But her mouth felt dirty, so she tried rubbing paper on her teeth but that was no help. She was at that age where she was aware of her appearance, so if her clothes were not right or her teeth looked dirty, it made her self-conscious and unhappy.

The children and their father arrived by taxi at a large drab grey school building, which blended with the grey sky above their heads. They could not believe what was waiting for them in that school. It was such a contrast with the bright open classrooms they were used to at home. Some teachers were dressed in long dark clothes, while others wore the brightest-coloured clothes they had ever soon. Some of the little schoolgirls wore long dresses with a headscarf on the back of their heads which reached down to their shoulders, while others wore their long dark hair loose down their backs, along with shorter dresses, making the whole situation very confusing.

Jonathan was brought into one of the classrooms, still crying for his mother. He could not understand a single word anyone was saying because they were speaking in Punjabi. Orla picked up a few words here and there because her father had taught her some Punjabi words during his day visits with the children. But she had never expressed any interest in learning to speak the language.

Most of the children did not speak to Orla and Jonathan, except for one little girl. Her name was Aisha and she sounded quite different, as if she was from someplace else – like them. She didn't speak much of her father's language either. Both girls got on well for the first few weeks and then one day Orla went to school and her friend wasn't there anymore. Orla had no idea what had happened to her. Maybe she went back home to her own house in another country she thought, and she felt lonelier than ever.

The toilets in the school were as bad as the ones in her father's house and everyone had the same lunch, which she could not eat very much of without her stomach turning. She prayed to God every day that she could go home to her mother but she didn't know if God was listening to her prayers. Her father had told her she was a bad girl but she didn't understand what it was that made her so bad. Maybe it was because he had taken her away from her mother and she wanted to go back home she thought to herself.

The children's grandmother could hardly speak any English so they couldn't communicate with her very well. She always had a cross look on her face and never hugged them, but seemed afraid of something all the time.

Their father's brother, Ahmed, hardly spoke to either of the children. He looked odd and he just kept stammering, which stopped him communicating with them altogether after a short time. Orla was not afraid of him but even at her young age she pitied him when she saw how her grandfather and father treated him.

No one read to them like their mother and Nana Bridget had done. There was no television in the house, just a radio. Most nights the children clung together in fear and cried themselves to sleep.

Orla was afraid of her father's mother, her grandmother Abeer. She wore heavy dark clothes and had her long grey hair tied up in a bun. Her mouth was permanently turned down, she looked cross all the time and her skin was dry and wrinkled. She got a better look at her grandmother when her headscarf was off. She watched as she took out her false teeth and put them into a big mug on top of a black cupboard each night. When the light was very low, Orla studied her grandmother's shadow on the walls and thought that she looked like a big black crow, which frightened the wits out of her even more.

Her grandmother in Ireland didn't have false teeth, and they had plenty of light coming in through the large windows in their house. She felt a pain in her heart as she looked at her father's mother without her teeth and she felt she must be over a hundred years old.

She felt utter despair now, with no hope of ever getting her life back or seeing her mummy or anybody else at home. Pure fear took hold of her and her young brother – and mixed with a strange resignation, she felt that this was the way their lives would be from now on.

Her father was watching her reaction from across the hallway and reached out and struck her with force across her left ear.

'Don't stare at your grandmother like that! She's a better person than you are – you're a half infidel, Fatima,' he said, bringing the child back to her sense of fearful reality.

Her ear hurt and she bit back tears of pain. She knew better than to answer him back or to let him see her cry. He shouted to her to turn her face the other way, and then hit her again.

Orla was old enough to know that she needed to wash regularly and did not want to go to school smelling as badly as the rest of the family. She asked her father if she could have a bath a couple of times a week before school, but Abdulla flew into a rage.

'You are not in Ireland now. That bitch you call your mother has spoiled you and your brother. That's all over for the two of you now. From now on, you will live like the rest of us.'

Jonathan wet himself most nights and often received a hiding for it. Orla told her father that she didn't know what was wrong with him, as he had never wet his bed at home.

'What do you mean "at home"? This is your home now!' He slapped his young daughter again, leaving her huddled and sobbing in a corner of the dark room.

She tried to wash her brother with cold water before he went to school and he tried to push his sister away. She was afraid that if he smelled bad, nobody would want to sit beside him. Although she wasn't yet nine years old, she had the maturity of a thirteen-year-old.

'Listen, Arsalan,' – she was afraid to call him Jonathan in case someone heard her and then she would be in trouble again – 'I could take you to the toilet every night before we go to sleep and it might stop you wetting the bed. I will go as well, so you won't be afraid. And then Daddy won't hit you for wetting the bed anymore.'

CHAPTER 36

Sean's recovery begins

At 5.30 on Tuesday morning, the house phone rang. Bridget struggled to answer it, afraid it might bring bad news at such an early hour. She held onto the back of the chair in the hallway to steady herself as she picked up the receiver, knowing she must be strong for everyone.

'Sean has just regained consciousness,' she heard Liam shout down the line in excitement. 'Can you believe it! He's even looking for a Coke!'

'That's the best news I have ever heard,' said Bridget, her body relaxing for the first time in weeks as she was overcome with joy and relief.

That day, candles were lit in the local church and in the hospital's little chapel in thanksgiving for Sean's recovery.

Later that day, the consultant neurologist, Mr Robert McKinsey, called the family into his office and explained to them that while it was good news that Sean had regained consciousness, his full recovery was going to be a slow process. He had received a serious trauma to his head and it was too soon to tell whether or not he had suffered any permanent brain damage. Sean was scheduled for a brain scan and they would know more after the results of that were available.

Bridget rang J.P. and told him everything that the doctor had told them about Sean's progress.

'Well, what do you think? she asked, waiting for his reaction.

'Did he get his scan results yet Mum?' asked J.P.

'We are just waiting on the scan now to see if everything is alright.'

After waiting for a further two days, Sean finally got the scan done on his head.

The result came back and the doctor spoke to the family. He said that unfortunately Sean had a minor brain injury, but with a lot of rehabilitation work, he would be alright in time. For the moment, his speech would be a little slow, as would be expected, and he had to be helped in and out of the bed and taken to the toilet.

'It will take a while but we are confident that he will make a good recovery. The medical team is happy with everything for now: he is making progress slowly. We will have to arrange some speech therapy to be put in place and whatever else he needs.'

Sean's mother spoke to J.P. again following the brain scan.

'Sean needs to get his life back on track: he is still in his teenage years with a lot of living still to do,' she said, confident that nothing else was going to show up in any further tests.

'Sure didn't God let him live for us J.P.?' she said, with emotion creeping into her voice.

She then handed the phone over to his father who told J.P. that the Garda had been in touch to let him know that they might have a lead on Sean's attacker.

'A witness had been getting into her car when she heard a commotion near the laneway where Sean was found. She saw two men arguing and one had what she thought was a hammer or some other weapon in his hand. She didn't believe they were local and maybe not even Irish.'

J.P. was arranging to take some time off work: he needed to get home to his family for a short stay and reassured his parents that he would be in Galway within the coming few days.

CHAPTER 37

The children flee Abdulla

Orla just could not take it any more … all the punishments for nothing and his constant anger. She simply could not understand why her father hated her so much. He was cruel to her brother also and to her poor Uncle Ahmed, who could hardly speak. There were awful rows between her father and her grandfather every day over her and her brother, and an air of permanent tension and fear. Are we not behaving ourselves and being good, doing as we are told by him? It seemed nothing would ever satisfy Abdulla.

Although only a young child, Orla was very intelligent, plucky and resourceful. She had been thinking of running away for a while and felt the following night was the time to leave. She and her little brother had to get away from this uncaring cruel house; she only hoped God would mind them on the way. After all, she told herself, if they stayed nothing was going to change, but if they went they might have a fighting chance of getting back home to Ireland, somehow.

A perilous journey lay ahead for the two children and Orla knew she would have to face terrible consequences if they got caught. She wondered if they would survive such an ordeal in this strange and alien country.

The children were in their bedroom. Orla was secretly putting some edible food she had taken from the kitchen into a bag.

'Shush, Jonathan, you have to be very quiet. This is going to be a big adventure for us, but you can't tell anybody or we won't be able to go. But if we do escape, then Daddy won't be able to smack us anymore and we need to try to get back to Mummy again. Wouldn't that be better for the two of us?'

The little boy stayed perfectly still and nodded his head, afraid to move in case they were caught. Orla stuffed clothes under their blankets in case anyone checked on them during the night. The children waited until everybody was asleep and then they crept out of the house and down a narrow road in the dark. They kept off the main roadways so that they would not be easily spotted by anyone.

They kept walking until they saw daylight, all the while terrified of getting caught.

They walked a very long distance and managed to get very far away from that cruel dark house where they had been so unhappy. They stopped behind a high wall and ate some of the bread and fruit they had taken, hidden from view, sitting down and resting for a while. Jonathan started to cry. 'I want to go home to Mummy now,' he wailed.

'Shush now, we're going home soon but we have to keep walking. You're a big boy, you can keep going, can't you?'

The children soon found themselves close to what looked like a huge rubbish dump. They had walked a long distance, but they were still only on the outskirts of Lahore. There they met a boy called Raham who told them exactly where they were. He was a young boy, probably around eleven years old or a little more, and was part of a group of street children who lived on their wits, without parental control. He was curious about these foreign children being on their own in such a place.

'Who are you?' he asked in Punjabi. Orla understood some words and tried to explain to him as best she could about her cruel father who had taken her and her brother from their home in Ireland, a place far away from here.

'Don't worry! We do what we can to survive out here. There are hundreds of us children and nobody cares about us. We just live on our own and manage for ourselves.'

'What do you mean?' asked Orla.

The boy told them that he would introduce them to his friends and soon they would see how they lived. He invited them to watch and learn from them while they planned their escape out of Pakistan.

'But don't talk to any adults or you won't get back, so hide when you see them. And when we're in the city, you will learn from us. Just don't get caught!'

Orla listened carefully but was somehow worried. On the other hand, she felt this friendly boy could be a great help to them. They were a long way from the airport. How would they ever get there?

Raham told them about 'Sister Mary', a good lady who kept a watch out for any new babies who were abandoned in the rubbish dump. He brought babies to her and she had sisters who took them to safety in a local convent. When they were old enough, these children would be put into an orphanage and in some cases put up for adoption. Raham was young but had an old head on his shoulders. He watched out for the younger children in the dump and taught them all he knew about how to survive.

Meanwhile, a furious Abdulla ran into the local police station, pushing everyone aside who crossed his path, shouting that his children were missing. He shouted even louder at the senior-ranking policeman who was the unfortunate person who met him when he arrived.

'What are you going to do about my missing children?' he kept shouting.

'Stop it right there sir,' commanded the inspector. 'Who gave you the right to come in here and start shouting at us like that?'

He told him to calm down and not to be so bloody rude and aggressive or he would find himself locked up in one of the cells downstairs.

'Now you must start at the beginning sir, so we can make out what all your howling is about. Do you understand me? We need to get some relevant information to help us to find your children, so please give me all the details.'

Abdulla told him about his wife in Ireland, the children's mother, being very careful to provide an edited version of the story and only the details he was prepared to give the police.

The police inspector told him that he should have known that relationships like his seldom worked out because they were a union of fundamentally different cultures with little in common. He added that with a huge amount of mutual respect, such marriages could work, but that it was very unusual for that to happen. He felt Abdulla was a stupid fool who clearly did not see things that way, as he continued to shout about his rights, displaying no respect for the children's mother back in Ireland.

Abdulla was so angry, he could hardly be calmed down. 'It was all her fault,' he said. 'If she had obeyed me, we would still be happily married and my children would not be missing.'

'But would you be willing to bring your wife over to Pakistan and promise to treat her well?' asked Inspector Shahbaz Nadeem.

'You must find my children now,' insisted Abdulla, ignoring the policeman's proposition. Abdulla was thinking at the same time that if he had another chance with Siobhán he would indeed bring her over to his homeland and that she would never return to Ireland. He would see to that. Treating her with respect was an idea that would never cross his ignorant mind.

Shahbaz Nadeem stared at the angry little man in front of him and thought that he did not deserve any help whatsoever, although the welfare of the young children had to be investigated as a matter of urgency. Having listened to Abdulla's account of things, he believed that he had beaten this young woman and was now paying a high price for his anger and stupidity. So the inspector thought that he would do as little as possible for Mr Hussain, whom he regarded as an idiot who was reaping the rewards of his angry and perverted actions. He wondered if people in Ireland saw this little monster of a man as a true representative of the proud and decent people of Pakistan.

The inspector started to pick holes in the edited description of events that Abdulla was putting forward as he tried to extract the truth from his story about the background to the children who had fled from his clutches.

'Tell me the truth – how did all this come about?' he demanded. 'Why did you take the children in the first place from their mother? Were they not happy? What did you do to the mother of your children that the marriage ended as it did?'

'She had to know her place,' Abdulla said. 'She was having trouble remembering who her boss was. I only wanted to teach her our ways, what was expected of her once we were married. So she needed to be disciplined to keep her in her place and to teach her to show me some respect. I was entitled to take what was mine in our marriage bed. After all, she belonged to me,' he raged as he spilled everything out to the inspector.

'Nobody belongs to somebody else,' the inspector told Abdulla. 'They might be in our care but we don't own them. How long did your courtship last before the two of you married? Did she get to know what kind of life she was letting herself in for? After all, her culture is so different to yours. Was she ready to learn our ways, learn the Quran, wear our clothes to cover up her body and respect our laws? Did she want to change her religion, to convert to our beliefs? If she did not, then she wasn't the right choice for a wife and she wasn't yours for the taking. You're just a barbarian, you stupid man!'

He wiped his brow, exasperated at dealing with this moron who had barged into the station demanding his rights, while two little children had felt compelled to run away from him because of his ignorance and cruelty.

'Will you check with the airport authorities to see if they have boarded any flights to England?' demanded an angry Abdulla. 'Isn't that what the government pays you for?'

'Actually it's not. Everybody takes part in a search for missing children. So you had better head out to the airport yourself, while we see what we can do at our end,' said the inspector, brushing Abdulla off and not lifting his head as he continued to write his notes while still talking to him. He would not show Abdulla the respect that his flawed ego demanded.

A full-scale search was put into motion that day, starting at the children's school. Everybody was worried for them. The teachers had not seen anything out of the ordinary happen in or around the school. They did not know who their friends were, so they questioned all the children.

Abdulla rang his shady friends in Ireland after a couple of days and asked them to check if his children had returned there. They checked out all the likely places around where the family lived in Galway, but could find no evidence of their return.

CHAPTER 38

The horrors of life on the street

Raham kept an eye on the two newcomers and taught them how to scavenge for food. They quickly learned the ways of the street children. It was going to be extra hard to forage a living for these two. Orla was always worried for them both and was terrified her father would find them and take them back to his home – anything was better than that she thought.

They first encountered the shocking reality of street life when they were out looking for food. One day, they were deeply shocked to find a tiny living baby in a sack. But Raham came to the rescue and took charge of the situation and put the infant in a safe place for the attention of Sister Mary, who knew exactly what to do with these little babies who had either been abandoned by their mothers who had no money or by those unmarried girls who wished to avoid bringing shame on their families. Such finds were a regular occurrence in the dump. That experience left a deep and very disturbing impression on Orla and her young brother. Such horror filled her with fear for her brother and herself. How could she protect them both in such a hopeless place?

Sister Mary was tiny, barely five feet in height, but she dedicated her life to the welfare of street children. Each morning, she made her way to the dumps, along with two other nuns, and they collected any abandoned babies. She had taught Raham English, and how to read and write, so he could read street signs and newspaper headlines. Being very bright and well informed, he was the perfect person to help other lost children. Ever since Sister Mary joined the convent, her heart had been dedicated to the children of the slums. She believed that adults always had a fighting chance of survival in such a cruel and uncaring world but the lost children had little chance; she and other social workers were their only lifeline.

Streetwise young Raham looked out for the welfare of the smaller children and fought their battles against pimps, child slave trade criminals and the hostile officials of the city. He managed a whole underground survival system. At night some of the children slept in underground slums, which were fairly safe places at night.

The two Irish children washed themselves in the Ravi River. All the children who lived in the dump washed there, and they had no choice but to do the same and they were glad of it.

'It's only for a short time till we get home to Mummy,' said Orla, who knew that they needed to leave Pakistan quickly as they could not live like that for very long without suffering the awful consequences and dangers of street life.

Raham tried to take the newcomers everywhere with him and taught them how to survive. Most of the children slept for a few hours during the day and then went out at night to the city to scavenge in the bins for reusable items such as plastic bottles, which the older boys could sell. They were warned to be careful of broken needles, blades and glass.

Of course, Raham could not protect them one hundred per cent of the time. Just when Orla thought they were safe, she was pulled down to the ground from behind one night and brutally attacked by a man dressed in white clothes, wearing black and white shoes. She noticed that his front teeth were missing as she tried to get away from him.

All the while, her brother was screaming for her some distance away. After a few minutes, the man went away, laughing at how easy it was to have his pick of these dirty street children. Orla could only understand some of what he was saying but she felt sore and confused and did not really understand that in fact she had just been raped. She recognised the man from being around some school children she had seen earlier dealing drugs around the dump.

Orla learned fast from her devastating experience. Survival was key, and it taught her the harsh lessons of life a long way from home. So they settled uneasily into their new way of living.

'Well, anything is better than Daddy shouting and beating us all the time,' Orla told her brother, who was finding life more than a little challenging at his tender age.

Life had been chaotic for Orla and Jonathan since they had been taken away from Ireland. Jonathan asked Orla one day when they were searching for food if she could find a chip shop like home for sausages and chips and an ice cream milkshake.

'Can we walk there?' he asked her innocently. 'Is it a long way away?'

With his little pleading eyes looking for some sort of normality, he was breaking his sister's heart. How could she explain to her young brother that they might never see their mummy again! She just knew that was a conversation she would never have with Jonathan, but deep down she felt they might be lost forever.

CHAPTER 39

A rescue plan takes shape

Liam, Bridget, J.P. and Siobhán were invited into the office of consultant Robert McKinsey in Galway to discuss Sean's progress. The results of the second scan were available and it seemed that the attack had caused a bleed to his brain that was not clear in the first scan. This had caused him to have a slight stroke. With physiotherapy and encouragement, he would probably get his life back to some sort of normality, but they would all have to spend a great deal of time helping him. And that was what his family and friends dedicated themselves to doing.

J.P. had arrived home for a week to see what progress Sean had made since his last visit a couple of months before. Sean's speech was slow, he still needed some help getting in and out of bed and sometimes he didn't make it to the toilet in time, much to his distress.

His family reassured him that he would get better with time and that he must have patience. J.P. encouraged him to work hard with the family, telling him that he would recover and then he would take him over to London for a long holiday.

'It will be great for you to get away after all you've been through Sean,' said his excited big brother, trying to lift his young brother's spirits.

Sean was visibly upset when he learned that the children were missing. He blamed himself for liking Abdulla and trusting him like he was a good friend.

'He completely fooled me,' said Sean. 'I should have paid heed to all your warnings Siobhán.'

'Don't be upset, Sean. Everyone was beginning to trust him. After all, the lying monster had said many a time how sorry he really was for upsetting Siobhán and the family,' said his father, trying to further reassure him.

J.P. felt that he had to set the wheels in motion to get the children back and now was the time to plan for that.

'We are going to get the children back somehow and hit him where it's going to really hurt him most. He needs to feel the pain that you have been through.'

So J.P. and Siobhán started to make a plan to rescue Orla and Jonathan. J.P. had a dark complexion, and he decided to exaggerate that by growing a black beard.

Meanwhile, Abdulla's former friend, Amahil Zakie, who now detested Abdulla, was very eager to help with the plan.

Amahil decided to teach J.P. and Siobhán some Punjabi and some verses of the Quran that would help them to put their plan into operation. In the meantime, Siobhán prepared to move back over to London as they worked out the details of the rescue.

CHAPTER 40

The runaways are discovered

Orla and her brother survived practically on their own for a long time in the slums. They had no means of counting the days or weeks but it felt like a lifetime for the two young children.

Raham was always moving around and they were fearful when he was out of their sight. He had told them to hide as much as they could from adults, but that was not always easy, as they had to make some sort of a living and scavenge for food. The weather was getting a lot cooler and they were looking for paper or anything else they could find to put around them to keep warm at night.

One night as they tried to sleep underground, Orla and Jonathan were awakened by the sound of a child screaming pitifully. Orla knew that they must stay out of sight and held her hand over her frightened little brother's mouth and told him to keep very quiet.

She peeped out and saw two young boys of about nine or ten years old who were running as fast as they could and were being chased by a tall, bearded man. The two boys were suddenly on the ground and all Orla could hear was moaning. She then realised that the boys were being beaten up for the proceeds of their hard day's work collecting valuable rubbish and that the man had taken everything they had from them. They were crying hysterically and the incident struck fear into all the street children in the vicinity.

Orla and Jonathan clung to each other. What were they going to do now? They had had enough of life in the slums. That horrible incident proved without doubt that they might not survive there much longer, so Orla decided that their only option was to try to get home to their mother somehow. They would have to walk to the airport as soon as possible, she decided. If they arrived at the airport filthy and smelling like street children, the airport people might not let them on a plane, thought Orla in her innocence, so they went and washed in the river to freshen themselves up as much as possible.

They headed off in the direction of the city, carrying some clean water and scavenged food for the journey. They planned to watch the sky and follow where the planes were taking off and landing. After what seemed like a very long time walking along one road, they still had not seen or heard any planes and it was beginning to grow dark.

Two local men, Nabeel and Shabaz Bibi, saw the two children on the side of the road and stopped their lorry to check on them. It was unusual to see young children walking along the road by themselves, especially at night.

'Where are you going?' Nabeel asked the frightened children. Orla and Jonathan hadn't time to hide – they were caught out and had to reply.

'We're looking for the airport. We need to go home to Ireland, to our mother,' said Orla.

'Well, come on and we'll ask a policeman to help you.'

The children were afraid to get into the lorry, thinking that maybe these men were bad people too. Orla could sense a feeling of panic rising inside her.

'Don't worry,' said Nabeel reassuringly. The frightened children reluctantly got into the lorry, with Jonathan holding onto Orla's hand so tight that his sister thought he would never let her go. The two kind men drove them to the nearest police station to find that their photographs were pinned up on a noticeboard there.

'There is a huge search going on everywhere for you two! Where have you been?' said the friendly policeman on duty.

'We have been living in the dump with some street children and then we decided to walk to the airport,' said Orla, 'because we are trying to find out way back to our mummy in Ireland.'

'Well let me telephone your family. I'm sure they'll be delighted to get you back safe and sound.'

The children were delighted, thinking that their mother might be coming from Ireland to collect them.

The policeman handed the children a bar of red soap and a brown towel and sent them into the toilets to clean themselves up.

They scrubbed their faces and hands till they were as clean as possible, but Orla knew that they still looked dirty – just like all the other street children.

When they came back into the room the kind policeman gave them a milky drink and some fresh bread, wondering why these children had run away from home in the first place.

CHAPTER 41

Abdulla brings the two home again

Abdulla had everyone he knew searching all over Lahore and beyond for the missing children. He did not care about his daughter but promised she would pay the price for kidnapping Arsalan. If anything had happened to her, he reasoned, his precious son would also be lost forever. So all his relatives had been searching the city and the waste dumps outside the city limits.

Over a few weeks, the family and friends spoke to a lot of street children during the search, but no one seemed to know anything about the missing children. Most of the children held onto their secrets – an unspoken rule amongst them. Raham knew they were bound for the airport, at least that was what they had told him when he first met them. When asked, Raham said he could not remember seeing any strange children around, meaning not from his country. He hoped in his heart they had achieved their miracle and had escaped without anything awful happening to them.

Abdulla then started to believe the children were back in Ireland. He relayed his fears to his parents and asked if they thought the same.

'It might be possible the children were taken out of the country so your hunch could be right, Abdulla. You go back to Galway, son, and see if you can find the children there. The sooner the better – they are part of our community now and are being reared in their father's faith so don't waste any more time.'

At ten o'clock on Saturday night the phone rang as Abdulla was preparing to leave for Ireland.

'Abdulla, answer the phone, it might be some good news,' said his father impatiently.

'We have found your two missing children,' said the policeman from the station where the children were. 'You must be thankful to Nabeel and Shabaz Bibi, who found them wandering along the road at the edge of the city, looking for their mother.'

'Thank you so much officer,' said a very relived Abdulla. 'We are so happy with this news. We will come to your station to pick them up as soon as we can. We should be there in about an hour, hopefully a bit sooner if the traffic is not too heavy.'

So his daughter had told the police she wanted to go back to Ireland. He wondered just what else she had told them. Well, she will pay a high price for the danger she has put my son in, he thought as he prepared to leave for the police station.

CHAPTER 42

Orla faces the wrath of her father

Orla hid behind the tall burly policeman, her heart beating hard when she saw her father and grandfather enter the station. Jonathan hid behind his sister and asked where Mummy was and when she would be coming for them.

'Well here they are Mr Hussain, safe and sound after their long ordeal. All they need now is a warm bath and a change of clothes.'

'Thank you, officer,' said Abdulla, reverting to his charming demeanour. 'I cannot thank you enough. We will be forever grateful to you for finding our precious children.'

'Don't thank me, thank the good people who found them and brought them here safely to the station. You owe them a big debt of gratitude.'

Abdulla pulled out a large quantity of rupees and reluctantly handed the money over to Nabeel and Shabaz Bibi, who accepted it gratefully.

Both children were stiff with fear, knowing that the vision of seeing their mother in Ireland had sustained them through the awful experience of living on the city dump, but now that dream had come to nothing. The kind-faced policeman saw things differently and said goodbye warmly to the children, hoping they had learned a hard lesson, but were now happy to be on their way home.

'Where did the two of you get to?' demanded a plainly irritated Abdulla. 'And what do you mean, leaving in the middle of the night like that, having everybody worried sick about you? Well, what answer have you got for me Fatima?'

'We just wanted to go home to Mummy,' said his trembling daughter, who was so nervous and frightened that she vomited onto the station floor.

Abdulla immediately offered an apology to the officer. 'Give her a cloth and she will clean up her mess,' he said with disgust.

'No,' said the policeman. 'We have someone who will do that. Besides, the little girl must be sick and very upset after all she has been through. Where is your compassion for this poor little daughter of yours?'

Once outside and away from the door of the station, Abdulla made it clear that he was their father and they were back with him now.

'How could you do this Fatima? My son could have been lost forever. Who gave you the right to take my precious son from his home and expose him to the dangers of the outside world?'

He pulled her up by her sore ear until she cried with pain, Abdulla almost frothing from the mouth with anger.

His mother then intervened and told him to leave the child alone.

'You cannot treat my grandchild like that. You need to show her some respect. The two children have been through a lot of hardship in the last few weeks and all you can think about is yourself,' she said, her voice full of anger against her abusive son.

The child held onto her grandmother's skirt, afraid to let her go. It was the first time that she had shown any kind of care or affection towards her.

Jonathan looked over at his sister and wanted to kiss her, like he did all the times when he was frightened and lost, but he knew that he would annoy his father more if he did. Abdulla continued his rant against Orla, again telling Jonathan that he could have been lost forever, and if he had been, it would have been entirely Fatima's fault. He also told the little boy to stop listening to stories about their mother in Ireland, telling him that it was all a pack of lies and that his mother had never cared for him or his sister. Jonathan listened but said nothing.

CHAPTER 43

A daring plan is perfected

Siobhán and J.P. worked hard to learn Punjabi and, with the help of a man in England who knew Siobhan's Uncle Tim, they had false passports made for themselves and the two children.

The man producing their passports and travel visas in England was an expert on how these things worked and was able to anticipate any problems that might arise along the way, especially at airports. Security was so strict and it was in his interests to ensure they did not get caught using these illegal documents.

They needed the false passports for the four of them to travel out of Pakistan, using false names, with J.P. and Siobhán posing as the mother and father of the children. The plan was to travel from New Delhi Airport in India – just across the Pakistani border from Lahore – and then on to London, before taking the final flight home to Ireland.

Uncle Tim had to forget his conscience about commissioning forgery in this critical situation and leave matters in the hands of Siobhán and J.P. to expedite the plan. He was troubled that he had to take this action, but could see no alternative. In all his years in the Garda, he never compromised himself and left with good references, and no stain on himself or his family, but he was glad now to be able to play a critical role in seeing the children returned safely from the evil hands of Abdulla.

J.P., Siobhán and their friend Amahil planned carefully how they would grab the children from outside their school in Lahore. First,

Amahil needed to hire a van. All his family were native Pakistanis from Islamabad, so he would not attract any suspicion. He would park the van at the side of the school and when he was finished using it, he would organise to leave it with a friend who would return it to the hire company. That would help to avoid any undue attention from the police if there was a subsequent investigation.

J.P. and Siobhán had to learn the basics of the Quran, so that if they were asked about it they would be well versed in its teachings. They found it hard and laborious work but it had to be done if they were to have any chance of getting the two children back safely.

J.P. and Amahil examined maps of the area where Abdulla lived, looking particularly at all the schools in the vicinity. Amahil would spend a couple of days going to each school to find the right one and to see who collected the children each day. He would watch their movements from the school to their house and, when the time was right, they would put their daring plan into action.

Siobhán dyed her blonde hair and eyebrows dark brown, and shopped for clothes suitable for a wealthy Muslim woman. It was important that she wore everything a Muslim woman would wear, right down to a pair of blue leather pump shoes. She learned how to wear the hijab properly on her head – she could not afford to let her guard slip – and was well versed in her new language. She was ready for the rescue and only hoped her nerves would hold up to the strain of this odious task ahead of them.

J.P. and Amahil bought the kind of smart clothes a Muslim businessman in Pakistan would wear. J.P. would act like a wealthy businessman, and be careful not to look out of place. Above all, he had to avoid catching the attention of the authorities.

J.P. collected the four passports from England. He was travelling under the name of Aariz Dhanial, Siobhán under the name Abida Dhanial, Orla was Arfa Dhanial and Jonathan would travel under the girl's name of Abina Dhanial.

J.P. and his sister would hand one passport each into their hotel and would still have another set in the event of having to leave their passports in the hotel later. So with every possible eventuality covered, they were ready to put their daring plan into action.

CHAPTER 44

A dangerous journey begins

J.P., Amahil and Siobhán boarded a flight from London's Heathrow to Benazir Bhutto International Airport, Islamabad. They took the train to Lahore and Amahil stayed with some relatives living close to the city. Siobhán and J.P. booked into the Arai Hotel in the city centre.

Amahil collected the rented pick-up van, along with a cover to put over the precious cargo he hoped to conceal in the back. He tried hard not to let his nerves get to him at the thought of the task that lay ahead. He met a close friend who helped him to put old cardboard boxes and bags of wood shavings into the pick-up to cover the occupants.

Siobhán had a couple of sets of suitable girls' clothes for her son and daughter if they needed to change. Jonathan and Orla would be told their new names when they were finally all together.

In the hotel, J.P. followed his sister to the reception desk. They handed over their forged passports and tried to remain calm.

'Yes, sir, your room is ready for you and your wife,' said the pleasant girl on the desk.

'Thank you,' said J.P. in convincing Punjabi.

'How long will you be staying, Mr Dhanial?'

'Well, quite possibly just a couple of days or maybe a week. We're meeting some family and after that we'll have a bit more clarity.'

The porter carried their luggage up to their room. J.P. gave the young man a tip and closed the door behind him. Siobhán flopped down onto the bed, overcome by the daunting task ahead of them. J.P. was trying to make himself appear relaxed and self-assured so as not to attract any kind of suspicion.

'Well, what should we do now?' said a worried Siobhán, knowing the dangers of the mission that lay ahead. J.P. suggested they have tea and discuss their next move, glad that all had gone smoothly till then.

They went down to the hotel lounge and ordered chai tea and coffee and acted as if they were on a short business break.

They flicked through copies of the *Business Recorder* and the daily paper *Nawa-i-waqt* and hoped their stay would only be a short one.

Amahil meanwhile checked out the schools, trying to find which one was attended by the two children. It took him three days but eventually he found the right school. He watched to see who collected them. Normally, Abdulla brought them to school and collected them, but he was away for a few days, so his mother was looking after them.

On the day Amahil located the school, he saw an old woman was waiting for them, but the following day they seemed to be finding their own way home. He was afraid they were being watched, so he kept himself well hidden. As they made their way out of the school, Amahil cautiously approached the children when they were some distance away.

'Are you Orla and Jonathan?' he asked them, trying to sound as friendly and kind as possible.

They looked very startled, but the young girl nodded. Jonathan hung on to his sister's arm, not quite sure what the man was saying.

'Were you being collected today?' he asked.

Orla shook her head. She was afraid of this stranger and did not know what to say or do, but she was glad that he knew their real names and that reassured her.

'Please trust me – I am Amahil and I am going to take you to your mum Siobhán, who is here with your Uncle P.J. They are going to take you home to Ireland. Don't say a word, just walk with me and be very quiet for all of our sakes.'

The children did as they were told, now feeling they could trust this kind-sounding young man who obviously knew their mother. They followed Amahil up a laneway and around the back of the school. He lifted them into the back of the pick-up and gently covered them up and told them not to worry, but they needed to be hidden until they were safe. As he was lifting Orla into the van, she asked him where her mummy was.

'You'll soon see her, Orla. She is here in the city and cannot wait to see you and hug you both.'

She was still a little apprehensive about trusting this stranger, but desperately wanted to believe that he was telling the truth.

In the van, Amahil changed his red top for a grey one, his green hat to black and his black pants for denim jeans. He painted one of his front teeth black with stage paint so he would not be recognised by any of the people around the school. He changed the number plate of the van, so if there was an SOS out for them, this would throw them off. Just before he drove away he phoned J.P. at the hotel from a public telephone box and spoke in code in case anybody was listening to his call.

'It's time we all met up with you and my family.'

'We're looking forward to seeing you. Listen, we're actually in the area now, so maybe you could meet me in the next few minutes? We'd love to chat over a couple of coffees if that was suitable for you both. Do you think you can make it?'

He delivered the lines he had rehearsed so many times so as not to raise any suspicion with the operator.

They had planned to meet up in a side street near the hotel.

J.P. had their bags packed and went down to the hotel reception to check out and pay their bill.

He thanked the hotel staff for their short but pleasant stay. Beside him, Siobhán thought that she would faint with nerves. She sipped her bottled water in an effort to keep upright, as the hotel receptionist handed over their passports to J.P.

'Is your wife feeling alright?' asked the receptionist. 'She looks quite pale.'

Siobhán managed to put a broad smile on her face. 'She's fine, thank you. Just excited at the prospect of meeting our family here.'

J.P. and Siobhán made their way to the agreed place where the van was waiting. They had been lucky in the hotel and nobody seemed to suspect a thing.

Now the race of their very lives was beginning! Before they left, Siobhán asked to take a quick peep in the back of the van at her children, but Amahil pleaded with her not to, as it was too dangerous and they had no time to spare.

Amahil drove as fast as he dared to his friend's house ten miles away. When he reached that safe house, he stopped the van and Siobhán jumped out and ran around to the back calling her children's names.

Orla jumped out, screaming with delight and disbelief at the sight of her mother, wondering why her hair was different under her scarf and why she was dressed like a lady from Pakistan.

'So that man wasn't a bad man after all Mummy,' said Orla.

Jonathan started to cry when he saw his mother, so she held him close, kissed him on the cheek and gave him her total reassurance. She told them they must have a wash in this house and then they would get dressed in new clothes for their journey home.

'Jonathan, your new name is Abina Dhanial. It's a girl's name, but it will be what you are called until we get home. You will be dressed up in girls' clothes for the journey home because we have to be very careful.'

The little boy agreed and even liked the idea of this adventure.

'You, Orla, will be known as Arfa Dhanial and your Uncle J.P. will be known as Aariz Dhanial, your father, and I will pretend to be his wife. My name will be Abida Dhanial. These are the names on our passports and who we are until we get back home safely to Ireland.'

After many tears and hugs with their mother and uncle, Orla's hair was cut very short again to try to disguise her. Soon the family were on their way, heading to New Delhi International Airport, the first leg in a nerve-wracking journey which just had to have a successful outcome.

They drove fifty kilometres to the border crossing at Kausus in Pakistan. Siobhán and the children were hidden under boxes and bags of wood shavings in the back of the pick-up and J.P. sat beside Amahil in the cab. At the border, Amahil spoke to the guards in their native language and explained that he was making a delivery of boxes and bags of wood.

Sweat rolled off Siobhán as she held her hand over Jonathan's mouth, afraid he might cough or sneeze with all the wood shavings around them. J.P. sat rigid with fear in the cab, because one wrong move and they would pay a heavy price, quite possibly with their lives.

The guard walked around the back of the truck and lifted the cover with his rifle, barely looking in before waving Amahil on.

Once over the border and out of sight of the guards, J.P., Siobhán and the children said goodbye to Amahil and boarded a train. They would be stuck on this very crowded train for four hundred kilometres – all the way to New Delhi International Airport.

There were a lot of soldiers on board, adding to the family's tension. The stink was desperate as the temperatures soared.

There was pushing and shoving on the train and people were tired and irritable from standing for a long time in the heat.

The children drank water and ate some bread on the long journey. The toilets were bad but Siobhán thought some of the toilets in their own trains back home were pretty bad, so toilets were the least of her worries.

J.P. held a newspaper, pretending to read it. Siobhán and the children didn't speak at all on the long train journey as they were afraid the soldiers or other passengers would recognise them as foreigners, and then their cover would be blown. One of the soldiers ordered an old man to get out of his seat, hitting him with his rifle as the old man struggled to stand up. The soldier sat down opposite J.P. He spoke to Jonathan, laughing, but the child could not understand him and froze with fright. Instantly, Siobhán explained in her practised new accent that the girl was mute and apologised to the soldier and no more was spoken between them till they reached their destination. J.P. and Siobhán tried to look confident, as if they knew where they were going on the next leg of their incredible journey.

Amahil was due to return to London on the next flight from Islamabad. After he had said goodbye to the O'Rourkes he drove to a secluded area of woodland and unloaded the boxes and wood. It would not do to have the same load on board when he crossed back in case he met the same guard on his return journey.

When he had returned the hired van, Amahil's friend dropped him at the airport in his own car. Now it was up to J.P., Siobhán and the children to give the performance of their lives as a married couple with their two daughters.

They were afraid that Abdulla might be waiting for them in the airport, but how could he have got there before them? J.P. reckoned he would definitely have gone to the Lahore airport to look if he was already searching for the missing children.

CHAPTER 45

Another search is organised

'Why did you let the children come home on their own from school?' Abdulla screamed at his mother. 'You know you can't trust Fatima, and now she's gone back to the dumps, to the street children again, hiding in the filth – and with my son, my precious son. What am I going to do now?'

'Let's all go to the dumps to search for them,' said his father, trying to calm his son down, although he was angry at Abdulla and thought he had brought all this on himself for leaving his homeland and not obeying him in the first place.

'See what trouble you have caused in my home – all because you went off and married an Irish girl and not one of your own kind,' Arslan said.

As his father lifted his hand in anger to strike his son, Abdulla put his hand up to catch hold of his wrist to show him that he would never control him by force anymore – that day was long gone.

'You listen, son,' said his exasperated father. 'We have been good enough to take these two children in when we shouldn't have had to, all because of the mess you have made of your life. And now you scream at your mother. I will not stand for this.'

Ahmed jumped in between his brother and father to stop them assaulting each other, but accidentally received a punch in the jaw from his angry father. Arslan was glad it was Ahmed he hit and not his prized but idiotic older son.

'Fatima should have known better,' said her grandmother, Abeer.

'I have saved her once but I will never interfere again. She is your responsibility and now look at all the trouble she has brought on all of us, including my husband and son. And now I am being blamed by you for causing this bad situation. I agree with your father. You brought all this on yourself.'

She explained to her angry son that she had just not been able to make the journey to the school that day and had hoped he would not find out.

'Why did you not ring me?' shouted Abdulla. 'I could have got Ahmed to collect the children. Why did you just leave them to do this?'

His mother thought that her granddaughter would never disobey her again, and after all, she pointed out, they had come home safely on their own the day before.

'She should never have tried to run away again, at least not until she is married off and is someone else's responsibility,' said an angry Abdulla.

Abdulla, his friends and family went out onto the streets again looking for the lost children, carrying photos of them. After hours of searching the dumps, there was still no sign of them.

'But they have got to be somewhere around here,' thought Abdulla. 'They would know their way around by now, having spent such a long time in the dumps with all the dirty street children the last time.'

CHAPTER 46

A hazardous journey home to a lovely reunion

A shiver ran down Siobhán's spine when she thought about all the enormous challenges they were facing in getting the children home safely from Pakistan. Feeling overwhelmed, she longed to be back in her childhood and safe in the protection of her much-loved parents; she wished she could just wake up and find that all this had been a bad nightmare. She hoped the airport staff would not find a problem with the passports. She felt the same fear as when Julie had dropped her at the train station all those years ago when she escaped Abdulla, but she knew that this situation was far more unpredictable and much more dangerous. She found it almost incredible that she was still being tormented by her former husband all these years later and that she had found it impossible to rid him from their lives.

The plane was not due to depart for another hour, so Siobhán and J.P. took the children to an airport café and ordered refreshments for everyone. They all tried to calm down with cakes and sweets for the children, but both she and J.P. knew they were still not out of danger by a long shot. In fact, the dangerous tests of their false documents and disguises were yet to come, so they both felt extremely apprehensive about the trip back.

Neither of them could relax. Siobhán felt worried sick and could barely get the tea past her lips. Her hands trembled and J.P.'s eyes roamed everywhere, looking out for any kind of possible threat. Finally, their flight number was called and everybody started to queue for boarding.

J.P. and Siobhán joined the queue and the children stayed very quiet, with Orla gently squeezing Jonathan's hand to reassure him. After they had checked in, they made their way towards the passport desk where an official examined their passports. They were asked to state what their business was in Pakistan and J.P. said they were visiting family, knowing he could give his friend Amahil's address if asked for proof. J.P. spoke fluently in Punjabi and the official looked the family over. They were dressed and looked like a wealthy Muslim family with their two daughters, with Jonathan acting out his part as a little Pakistani girl so well. Siobhán could hardly breathe with anxiety. Orla whispered to her to take a sip of water, which calmed her a little.

At last, they were waved on, but they were not out of the woods yet, because they still had to go through a security screening.

Suddenly there was an announcement for all passengers: 'For security reasons, all departing passengers will now have to submit their papers for examination again. Our apologies for this inconvenience.'

Some people were subsequently taken away for questioning, while everyone else was waved hurriedly on, but not before Siobhán almost fainted, attracting the attention of security staff. J.P. told them that she was expecting their third child and had not eaten any breakfast that morning. He was sorry the minute he had said this, afraid that they would get a doctor to check her and make sure that she was able to make the journey. He apologised for the concern that was caused about his wife as he helped Siobhán back onto her feet again. Siobhán managed to put on a brave smile, apologising for any hold-up caused, as the two frightened children looked on, still afraid to move out of concern for their mother. Finally, they were all allowed to board and allocated their seats for the journey to London.

How close were they from being told they could not fly! They could easily have been told to step aside until they were sure that Siobhán was well enough to travel, possibly missing their flight as a result and risking possible exposure.

Throughout the journey they knew they had to keep up their act of being the model Muslim family until they were safely off the plane, through passport control and safely back in England.

Within a few hours, they were finally able to breathe again, as they left the airport and made their way to the centre of London. They took a taxi to J.P.'s flat, where Jim and Marreese were waiting for them, having prepared a wonderful meal for all of them. Then it was time to relax after their ordeal – for the children, it was like a dream come true.

Orla and Jonathan told Siobhán about how bad life had been with their father and how they had escaped by foot at night to find the airport alone, but ended up in the vast city dumps as they foraged for food with the local street children. They described the horrors of street life and how they were later handed over to the police to be taken back to the cruelty of Abdulla again. Siobhán could hardly believe that her precious children had been subjected to such horrors, but was deeply touched by their burning desire to return to the love of their family in Ireland, away from the monster who had kidnapped them, just when all were feeling they could trust him.

J.P. described their incognito travels in detail, travelling as husband and wife with two young daughters under false passports. Jim and Marreese were amazed at how daring they had been and speculated about how they would have fared if they had been found out. J.P. was full of praise for his Pakistani friend Amahil who had managed to gain the confidence of the children and to guide them to safety from outside their school.

'Without Amahil we couldn't have pulled off the whole operation!' said Siobhán. 'Certainly the children would not be here in the safety of London. There's a good chance that otherwise they would have been lost to us forever, and would have been brought up by their savage father in a totally hostile and abusive environment. I was particularly concerned about Orla, who was constantly being punished by that beast of a father, who never wanted a daughter of his own.'

After hot baths and spending an emotional and relaxing evening with Jim and Marreese, they all went to bed on temporary camp beds covered with lovely soft white woollen blankets. For the children, it felt like they were in a very secure place – one of peace and kindness and love, after all their torments in Pakistan.

After breakfast the next morning, J.P., Siobhán and the children made their way to the airport to fly to Dublin, where they were welcomed by their overjoyed parents Bridget and Liam, along with Pádraig and their cousins. Pádraig was waiting patiently to give his wife a long heartfelt kiss and a dozen red roses, along with hugs and presents for the children.

Pádraig had spent some sleepless nights worrying about her, J.P. and the children. He had tried his best to keep positive for their parents' sake and to have hope throughout their ordeal, but Siobhán could see he looked a little gaunt from all the worry.

The news media had got hold of the story so the family decided to put off returning home to Galway, instead spending a few days in a Dublin hotel until things had quietened down a bit. They were joined from London by Trudy and Amahil and together they celebrated the end of the children's ordeal, the adventure of a lifetime for J.P. and his sister and the prospect of a happy life for all in Ireland. Siobhán embraced Amahil like she would her brother, and Trudy like a sister, while the children were all over this very special man who had encouraged them to get into the safety of the pick-up van; they knew that he would be in their lives forever.

CHAPTER 47

Orla's past comes back to haunt her

After all the euphoria surrounding the successful repatriation of the two children had died down, Siobhán, Pádraig, her mother, father and the children talked about the realities of their time in Pakistan. Jonathan spoke up first, saying that their daddy had beaten them a lot of the time.

'And Mummy, we were good, but he still shouted at us and he beat Orla nearly all the time, saying that she was a very bad girl. But she minded me, even when bad things happened to her in the dump with all the other children.'

Siobhán waited for Orla's story but she talked about everything and anything else – the poor dirty children and the abandoned and dead babies, but she would not talk in detail about what had actually happened to her during the time they were in the dump, living as street children.

When the time was right, after a couple of months of counselling for Siobhán and the children, they went back to school, but not everything that had happened to them was spoken about in the counselling sessions.

Orla spoke to her mother about her vagina being sore all the time and that bath water did not soothe it. She never spoke about it during the counselling sessions. Siobhán took Orla to see Dr Anne Lannigan and Siobhán explained what Orla had been through and asked that she have a check over.

After examining her, Dr Lannigan spoke to Siobhán in private and told her that Orla had a venereal disease. 'Did she tell you that she had been attacked and raped?'

Siobhán stood up and gripped the doctor's desk in shock. She told Dr Lannigan that her child could not have known what had happened to her and certainly did not know what rape meant. Both women spoke to Orla and asked her in more detail about what had happened to her in the dumps and slums of Lahore. Orla then admitted that 'bad men' had attacked her but she did not know what exactly they had done to her, except that it had made her sore. She tried to explain as best she could.

'That was during the first time we escaped when we lived on the dump for a long time and lots of horrible things happened. We also went away a second time and set out to walk to the airport, but two people picked us up and took us to the police station, and then Daddy came and took us back to his house, and he beat me very badly but my granny Abeer pulled me away from him just in case he tried to kill me.'

Siobhán was almost on her knees crying and the doctor was visibly upset about this young child's ordeal and relieved by how lucky the children had been to have made it home alive. Orla would only grasp the seriousness of the whole bad episode in their young lives when she was a lot older.

The doctor arranged for more counselling for both children and Siobhán. Jonathan eventually revealed their experiences of being afraid of the wild dogs and how they lived on the dumps. He spoke of how awful it had been in his father's house, how they were not allowed to wash themselves and how afraid he was of his father and afraid for his sister's life. He also revealed that he had started to wet his pants and the beatings that resulted from that. He described the cockroaches that crawled through the rice and how he had to wait for his grandmother to flick them away before he was forced to eat it.

It took over a year for the children to get back to any sort of routine. Orla was treated for VD, but Siobhán decided not to tell her what it was. In time she would, when Orla was a young adult.

Pádraig and Siobhán were closer than ever and she was able to relax fully in his trusting arms. She had never known such tenderness and real love. He helped her to see herself as a wonderful mother and a beautiful woman, whom he loved unconditionally. They were now a family and the children called him 'daddy'. Pádraig had put his name down as one of Orla's guardians, giving her his name for now, much to the family's delight. As their father was still alive he could not legally adopt her.

Sometime later, Abdulla returned to County Cork and went back to work for his Pakistani relations who lived there. His return was largely to do with pressure from his parents who could not stand his cruelty and warped view on life. He reverted to selling stolen merchandise, hooking up with his old pals again. He had decided not to bother searching for his children again, regarding it as too much trouble and not worth the effort. He had no idea how they had escaped from Pakistan.

But Abdulla knew where Siobhán lived, so the children were watched constantly. They were not allowed to walk anywhere alone, because the family never knew when and if Abdulla might turn up again – and if he didn't come himself, who he might send to try to kidnap them again.

Sean thankfully made a full recovery after about a year. With much hard work and physiotherapy he regained his full health. He too always looked over his shoulder, half expecting to find Abdulla or one of his cronies behind him, ready to attack him.

All of the family had paid a high price for Siobhán's innocent introduction to a young Asian man in London who could be full of charm, but who turned out to be a complete madman. He had cleverly reeled her into his wicked life and brainwashed her into thinking she was a worthless human being.

Five years went by and Siobhán still suffered nightmares. In her dreams, she was still with Abdulla sometimes and could not escape. Pádraig often woke her up when she cried in her sleep.

After the children returned from Pakistan, Siobhán gave birth to a new baby. It was a son and they named him Cathal. He was a much-wanted baby – Pádraig's son – and he completed their happy family. At that stage, Orla was just fifteen and Jonathan was eleven. Siobhán asked Amahil and Trudy to be Cathal's godparents.

Orla's very troubled past was catching up with her and she began to suffer panic attacks. Indeed, at times in her young life she was simply unable to cope. She had constant flashbacks to the dreadful years of torture suffered at the hands of her sadistic father. Her self-worth had suffered a great deal and at times she believed her father was probably right about her when he had said she was useless and not fit to live. He used to call her a mongrel dog, not fit for his family. He had told her that her mother's family did not want her either and that they too would treat her with contempt if they got the chance. She was not one of them, he had told her when he was giving her a beating for not being the boy he had always wanted. He had also said she was a waste of his hard-earned cash.

As a result, Orla chose friends who did not think much of themselves either. These were lost teenagers who had succumbed to substance abuse and antisocial behaviour. So Orla became caught in the same downward spiral, smoking and drinking excessively. At the same time, her poor performance at school was a major source of concern.

Pádraig tried to reason with Orla, encouraging her to find better friends and appealing to her to recognise the dangerous path she was on before it was too late. But Pádraig's gentle efforts had little success and Orla became very abusive.

'Fuck off and leave me alone. You're not my bleeding father. You've no right to lecture me – and I'm not your dutiful daughter, so fuck off out of my life!' Orla shouted at him.

'How dare you speak to Pádraig like that, Orla. He is trying to do his best to help you to lead a better life and to deal with the problems of your past,' said Siobhán. 'You cannot treat your family so badly. It's time we all went back to counselling as a family to see if they can help us to understand what's going on with you Orla, and maybe they can help us fix things. The counsellor will help us to understand what's happening in your head. Do you understand me, Orla?'

'No, I'm not going back to any counsellor, so you can fuck off too Mum. You don't understand a frigging thing about what's going on with me. I don't give a fuck what anyone else thinks! You weren't there to protect us when we needed you most. How could you even begin to understand how I feel?' She slammed the front door on her way out to meet her friends and to have her daily fix of coke.

By the time she was just seventeen, Orla's teeth were in a bad way as a result of her drug use. Siobhán was in despair about her weight loss too. At that stage, she was down to seven stone in weight, which was far too thin for her six-foot frame. Siobhán was at her wit's end to know how to deal with her. And she was at a loss to know where the money was coming from to feed her drug habit.

In one of their frequent rows, Orla told her mother that she would be better off dead. That was what she wanted.

'Why will you not listen to reason and take help when it's given to you?' said her mother.

'Why don't you fucking listen to me and leave me alone?' was her response.

Pádraig and Siobhán were at the end of their tether with her, and knew that something drastic had to be done. One evening they followed her from a safe distance when she left home and were totally shocked to see her going into a seedy hotel on the outskirts of Galway. They went in to see her going up the stairs with a much older man.

Siobhán and Pádraig burst open the bedroom door to see them both snorting coke before getting into bed for sex.

They grabbed hold of Orla and carried her out, kicking and screaming. When they got her home they told her to go to bed, despite suffering a torrent of verbal abuse from her. They then took turns to watch her throughout the night in case she self-harmed.

Next day they both tried to reassure her and to discuss her problems openly. They told her how much they loved her and that they were prepared to work with her to get her clean and hopefully to start to rebuild her life.

'Orla, please love yourself and see yourself as your family sees you and don't give into the lies that your father fed you. You are a wonderful young woman who has great potential and we all love you very much.'

Much to their relief Orla listened and told them how much she hated what she had become and that she knew she had to change to avoid complete self-destruction. The three of them knew it would be a long road ahead but were happy that Orla was realising that she had to put her past behind her at last.

CHAPTER 48

Orla's life is transformed

With much help from her family and her own personal resolve, Orla succeeded in time in turning her life around. By the time she was nineteen, she was starting her first year of college, studying for a degree in social work. She was still always on the alert, never walking down a dark passageway or lonely road alone. She avoided taking any chances with any aspect of her life. There was a time when she was too afraid to live, when she worried about getting caught up in a hopeless life of drink and drugs. With all the love and encouragement and professional help she had received, she knew deep down in her heart that nothing bad was going to happen to her again.

Her father had called her 'a worthless little bitch' so many times that she had truly believed his words. She might have died by his hand had his mother not stopped the beating and saved her. But now she was fully on the road to success. She bleached her dark hair blonde and wore jeans and sweaters with boots or wedge shoes. She made more of an effort to look like her trendy Irish friends, while blocking out the bad memories still churning around in her tired head.

When her studies were finished she planned to look for a job helping young children and babies in need somewhere. She was especially drawn to working with abandoned street children abroad and wanted to save as many young lives as was humanly possible, remembering how she and Jonathan had once lived as street children themselves.

It was not all plain sailing of course. There were the occasional relapses when she dabbled in coke and drinking, and she had difficulties in sustaining a long-term relationship with any boyfriend, but thankfully that was all receding into the past.

She worked hard at college for four years and after graduation she went to work with street children in Pakistan. She met 'Sister Mary' who was now getting a little old for her heroic work, along with the other nuns. She asked them what had happened to the brave young Raham. Thanks to the vision of 'Sister Mary', he too had turned his life around and completed his studies as a social worker. He had taken up residence in part of the convent and continued his charitable work with the abandoned children of Lahore and managed to transform as many young lives as possible. He was extremely glad to meet Orla again and to see how she had turned into a fine confident young woman who had also dedicated her life to the welfare of others.

CHAPTER 49

Jonathan's debt of gratitude

Even when he reached seventeen, Jonathan could still clearly remember the terrible things that had gone on in Pakistan when he was a young child there. He recalled what had happened to his sister in the dumps, although he tried not to think too much about what they had experienced there together.

He could not handle the thought that he had come so close to living over there for the rest of his life, and to the possibility of losing the sister he had totally depended on for support.

He knew how fortunate he was to have been snatched out of that awful place by his mother and uncle, along with their friend Amahil.

Jonathan loved his mother and Pádraig (whom he now regarded as his father) more than he could put into words. He always tried to help his sister like she had helped him when he was so small. He told Orla that he loved her very much, even though he found the words difficult to say. He found it hard to show that type of emotion as he grew older.

He was not sure what he wanted to do after he finished school but hoped he would go to college and make something of his life. He worried sometimes that he might turn out worthless, but at the same time he knew he had been given a second chance at life when it could have been so different. So he felt he needed to make every effort to repay his good fortune.

CHAPTER 50

Abdulla meets his end

One Saturday night at the end of September, Abdulla was on his way home after collecting money from the two men who ran his criminal operations. He liked to get his hands on his cash before they all met up later in his house for dinner and sexual pursuits. As usual, his new wife, Kim, would be ready for them and would have a good dinner prepared for the men.

He was driving slowly in torrential rain on a narrow back road he normally took on the way home. It was so heavy that he could not see the road clearly as his windscreen wipers tried to cope with the deluge.

Twenty minutes into his journey he saw through the rain what he thought were two figures with flashing lights and assumed it was a Garda checkpoint. He could hardly see out through the window but thought he should stop as he was keen to avoid any difficulties with the law in his adopted country.

He brought his car to a halt and opened the driver's door. He was immediately set upon by two men dressed in black with their faces covered. They pulled him from his car and demanded the money they knew he had on him. They had been following his movements during the day and knew he was carrying a large quantity of cash. Abdulla thought he could bully his way out of this confrontation, as he had done throughout his life. But the men beat him savagely and he found it impossible to defend himself from their vicious assault. In the course of the attack he fell to the ground, hitting his head on a rock at the side of the road. It was a fatal blow that cracked his skull.

As he lay dying, the two attackers pulled the money out of Abdulla's tightly gripped hand and made off with the cash.

A passing motorist saw the car with the lights still on and stopped to find Abdulla lying fatally injured on the side of the road and called an ambulance.

The paramedics could find no sign of life and pronounced him dead at the scene.

The Garda went to see his wife Kim to tell her the terrible news of her husband's death.

She took it surprisingly well, one of the Garda observed … not the usual response of a person who had just lost a loved one.

It was a case of history repeating itself. Kim felt completely liberated, knowing she had escaped the brute, the bastard who had made her life such a misery. Now she was free of that evil pig and free of those awful men who came there to exploit her body for his gain.

The good news of his death meant a new start for Kim and her son – a child she wished she had never had, but a son she had grown to love.

The minute the Garda had left her home, she locked all the doors and made sure the windows were tightly fastened and the curtains closed so Abdulla's 'friends' could not come in. She went upstairs and lifted the floorboard in their bedroom. It took the best part of the night to count the money – her money, which she had earned by the sweat of her brow. She counted €477,600 – enough for a fresh start. Kim would be able to sell this house of horrors and give a share of the sale to the other two children he had only spoken about a couple of times since she met him. She knew they lived in Galway somewhere.

She was still only twenty-eight. She had come from a poor background, a family with no money to fund her education, and so she had started working in a brothel all those years ago and saved for a better life. It was her misfortune to meet the charming Abdulla, to find herself trapped into a marriage that saw her ending up as his sex slave, just like Siobhán all those years before.

When it came to Abdulla's funeral arrangements she told his relatives over in Pakistan that he never gave her any money for herself – only enough to run the house and that was very little. When he died, there was very little money in his bank account.

Kim never told anyone about his hidden stash of cash of course. They could put that bastard in a pauper's grave for all she cared, and it was left up to his relations to take his body back to Pakistan and to sort out the arrangements for themselves.

Kim and her son moved away shortly after his death with the help of a good friend, as she tried to get her life back on track, well away from her former residence in County Cork. She instructed a local auctioneer to sell the house and gave him her new address and phone number, but she also told him that no matter who came looking for her contact details, he was not allowed to hand out that information. She worried that Abdulla's relations might try to take her son and had resigned herself to looking over her shoulder for a long time to come. She also decided to change her son's Muslim name to Justin, a name she had always liked.

After exhaustive investigations by the local Garda, nobody was ever changed with Abdulla's murder.

CHAPTER 51

The children, post-Abdulla

An old friend of Siobhán's from the hotel she had worked in down in County Cork rang her with the news about Abdulla's demise. Siobhán was pleased she would never have to anxiously look over her shoulder again. The brute was dead and her daughter and son, along with her extended family, would never have to worry about him again.

Siobhán was excited for a while and relished her newfound freedom. For a moment she thought she should feel bad about her former husband, but she could not feel the slightest sense of remorse. It felt good to know that he had received his just reward – the man who was a big black stain on her life. Now those black days had finally been removed forever.

Siobhán continued to worry about Orla and hoped that she would find lasting happiness. She wanted Orla to see herself as a valued member of her community and not to measure herself on what men thought about her. Her mother tried to convince her that there were decent men out there and that if she respected her body, they would respect her also. But Orla's response was always that she was far too young to be looking for a match.

For now, Orla had dedicated her life to helping young vulnerable children in need. That was a goal she had set herself a long time before. Her new life was working with Sister Mary's order amongst the street children of Pakistan. It brought happiness to her and her parents to know that she had finally settled down and found her true calling.

Siobhán was also anxious for her son, Jonathan. He was far too quiet and spoke little to anybody. He had a couple of good friends who were also quiet and reserved. She and Pádraig kept a close eye on him, hoping he would be able to express himself in a more outward way and not bottle up things that had happened in the past. Jonathan was quite different from his sister and tended to hide his true feelings. He and his sister were glad that their evil father was no longer a threat, but he remembered that his father had liked him much more than his sister and he had mixed emotions about his death. He wondered what his father's attitude would have been to him now that he was a young man? Would he have become his friend, or would he have been the same hostile figure he remembered?

He wondered why his father had not made the effort to come back for him after he fled Pakistan. Why did he forget him? At the same time, he was relieved that he hadn't been taken back forcibly to his father's homeland, to a house of bad memories and continued abuse. But he never forgot his father and struggled to understand his own feelings, which he sensed were confused and out of tune with reality. He understood that he would need some help in resolving these conflicting emotions.

CHAPTER 52

A surprise gift

One day, there was a big surprise for Siobhán's family when a letter arrived from Donald Davitt, a solicitor from Dublin, informing Siobhán that Orla and Jonathan had been left a sum of money from the sale of their father's estate and asking if they would come to his office to process the necessary documentation. Abdulla's second wife, Kim, had informed her solicitor about the two children from her husband's first marriage and decided that some justice needed to be done in their favour.

Siobhán could scarcely believe that she was going to get back some of her money – yes, her money – and that the children would benefit from his ill-gotten gains. She knew if the brute was still alive, he would never have given them a second glance, never mind money. So there was some justice at last from the madman who had taken everything, including her dignity and self-respect, and led her into a cesspit for all those years, taking a large chunk of her young life. 'Yes, some justice at last,' she thought.

Siobhán thought about his second wife, Kim. She was thankful for her generous heart in giving Siobhán's two children some money from their father's estate. She knew this woman must also have gone through hardship at the hands of that evil brute, but happily she was now free also, and she hoped for her sake that she would get far away from the bad memories, and that she too would find a decent man in the future.

CHAPTER 53

Sean finds love and marriage

Sean had met Hermine Higgins when he was twenty-five years old; by then, he was a fully qualified carpenter. Liam and Bridget were delighted, but at the same time a little worried for him. His personality had changed somewhat since his attack and coma. He was not the same happy, jolly young man that he had once been, although since he had met Hermine his life had changed for the better and Liam and Bridget could see the old Sean shining through again.

Hermine was a slim girl with brown eyes and long dark curls and had a vibrant personality. She was an only child and her parents were big farmers a couple of miles away. Liam said she looked a bit on the delicate side, like she wouldn't be much good for heavy farm work. He felt sorry for Hermine's family – not having a young man of their own to run the farm with them. Hermine was a strong young woman mentally, however, and played a major part in how the farm was managed.

'Looks can be deceiving,' Sean said to his father. 'Don't underestimate her capabilities!'

Hermine drove her jeep hard around the extensive farm, rounding up sheep along the edge of the local mountain range along with her clever sheepdog Max.

Sean spent more time down on the farm than at home, but his father was happy for him as he still also helped out on his own farm when needed. His life could have been a whole lot different and Liam thanked God for giving his son back his health.

Sean got on well with Milo and Maura, Hermine's parents, and they were glad to see him helping around the farm. After all, he was born into a small farm so he had plenty of experience. At last, they had a lad around who was not afraid to break a sweat and work hard to improve how the farm operated. Milo had met many a lazy lad on his farm throughout the years, so was glad that Hermine had such a strong man by her side, who would help to run the farm after their day. His daughter was a hard worker and had no problem managing a large herd of cattle or sheep. 'Don't let her slim build fool you. My daughter is as strong as an ox!' he said proudly to Sean.

There was excitement all around the area when they became engaged and planned to marry.

J.P., Jim and Marreese came over from London for the wedding, with J.P. acting as Sean's best man.

Trudy and Amahil also came over for the wedding, which was truly a family celebration for everyone. They had opened an Indian restaurant in the heart of London five years previously, after saving up every penny for a long time. So they made their dream of self-employment and independence come true, putting off having children until the time was right. When they arrived in Galway, Trudy was expecting her first child two months later. So the excitement level was high on Sean's big day with the prospect of a new baby on the way.

Amahil and Trudy asked Siobhán and J.P. to stand in as godparents along with Trudy's brother and sister at a local Anglican church near her parents' home in the south of England. Siobhán was very much looking forward to having a little holiday over in London – giving her a chance to buy something for her wardrobe and to enjoy London, knowing that her bad experiences there were now behind her forever.

Amahil arranged five days off as a holiday, putting George Loftis in charge. He had been working with Amahil and Trudy for four years, since he had arrived in London from Northern Ireland, and was one hundred percent trustworthy.

CHAPTER 54

Family matters after Abdulla's funeral

Abdulla's parents never came to grips with the difficulties they had had with him over the years – in particular, how he suddenly left them to go back over to Ireland after their grandchildren had disappeared. He never contacted them again and this upset them greatly. They felt he had used them and had brought trouble on their household with all the beatings he had given to his young children when he lived with them. Because Abeer had to listen to her grandchildren crying so much of the time, she had become depressed. She felt powerless, not being able to stand up to her son and her heavy-handed husband at such a late stage in her life. Arslan still ruled the house with fear and their son Ahmed was always at his father's beck and call, still afraid of him and subject to his anger and aggression.

The phone call from Ireland informing them of Abdulla's death had a profound effect on both parents, along with hearing the news that he had married a second time, to a woman called Kim, and had another child, a two-year-old boy. At the same time, there was no word about the two older grandchildren.

Despite all the havoc Abdulla had caused in the lives of so many people, his mother was horrified to hear of his death and mourned the son she loved. His father's reaction was one of disbelief and he directed his anger once again towards Abeer for bearing him a second son who turned out to be a halfwit.

Abdulla's family arranged to repatriate his body back home to Pakistan. His father was determined that he was coming home, no matter what it cost. Abdulla's relatives in Ireland were reluctant to help his parents, as Abdulla had been robbing them for a long time. They told Arslan that he had reared a very dishonest son and that Abdulla owed the company thousands of pounds; they were ashamed to call him a blood relative. Arslan could not believe, or would not believe, that Abdulla was dishonest – if he had taken a few things then they must have been paying him very little money for all his hard work. Arslan knew that Abdulla was a hard worker and in time he would set about clearing his son's name. In the end, Arslan raised most of the money and the relatives in Cork grudgingly gave over the remainder of the sum required.

Arslan was inconsolable over the loss of his elder son and it became very real when Abdulla's body was returned to his family. He had the body cremated and his ashes brought back to the house and placed on top of his best piece of furniture. Arslan laid his prayer turba on the floor in front of his son's urn and prayed for his soul.

His son was finally home where he belonged, with his family. His father also knew his son would not want to be back home, but it was a punishment he deserved. You will never go away again thought Arslan in his vindictive, evil, mercenary little mind. Yes my boy, we are seeing justice for me at last. You walked out on your father, but now I have you back. Arslan cried bitter tears for his lost son and himself, while feeling extreme anger at losing his prize, the son he was so proud of.

The next day, Abeer saw her husband walking out of the front door with the urn under his arm. He stopped for a moment and looked at his wife before continuing on his way, closing the door firmly behind him. He took a bus down to the railway station and waited for the train to take him to Punjab. He felt he had to get away from his demons. His heart was broken and he could not deal with the inferior son he was left with; any feelings he had for Abeer were long gone, along with her youth. He had stayed to rear his son Abdulla and to reluctantly provide for his second son Ahmed. But his work was done now. His pride and joy was now departed. He did not know what to do or where to turn next as he held his son's ashes under his arm.

The train pulled into the station and a mad dash was made to board by a crowd of surging passengers, leaving the elderly Arslan to scramble aboard. As the train was pulling out, he dropped the urn onto the train tracks. He tried to retrieve it but lost his balance and fell underneath the wheels of the train and instantly lost his life.

Abdulla's death was also a turning point for his brother Ahmed, who had finally had enough of the insulting names his father had called him since he was a young child. It was time for a new life … a new country. So he pulled together all the money he had saved throughout the years working for his father and decided to head to Ireland to work for his relatives in County Cork. Ahmed made a phone call to Ireland to let his relatives know of his intention to go there to work with them, assuring them that he would never engage in dishonest activities like his older brother had, but they told him not to bother. They told him that if Arslan could rear one dishonest son, why would the second son be any different? So poor Ahmed was condemned to remain in Pakistan.

CHAPTER 55

J.P. returns from London to build a business

J.P.'s mind had always been focused on his target. He had saved hard and, some years before, he had started investing on the stock market. In time, he became a very competent investor and saw his profits rise steadily. Within a few years he had made enough money to buy his own hotel and return to his beloved Galway.

He bought the Armond Hotel with a hundred bedrooms in Galway city. It was purchased in early February and he planned to have it ready for business from the last week in June. Siobhán was employed by him to ensure its success, as he wanted the business to be rooted in family ownership.

Up to then, Siobhán had been working as a part-time cook in a small local hotel, and was content with her lot, but following J.P.'s investment, she could see her horizons broadening.

Pádraig was by then well established in his architectural practice and could provide for Siobhán and the family. Orla and Jonathan's rooms were always there for them if they decided to return home.

J.P. advertised the hotel in the European and North American media, and developed connections with several other holiday providers, meaning he was in a very strong position to offer fully packaged holidays to prosperous customers eager to explore the attractions of Connemara and the west coast of Ireland.

The hotel had a large swimming pool with a spa attached. It also boasted a well-stocked gift shop selling the best of Irish crafts and luxury products, such as crystal and hand-woven traditional tweeds.

J.P. needed to put together a competent workforce to form the hotel's operational team, so he advertised widely for staff to run the bedrooms, kitchen, dining room, bar and restaurant, along with reception staff and porters.

He and Siobhán spent a couple of days going through the applications received and drew up a list of potential candidates.

One of the applicants was Gabrielle Ducill, who was born in Jamaica. She had a dark complexion, large brown eyes and long dark hair, set off by a cheerful and determined disposition. She hoped to be appointed to head up reception, drawing on her experience at the New York Hilton. She was petite and always smartly dressed and for the interview she wore a smart navy suit with a white silk blouse, black high heels and her trademark red lipstick.

Gabrielle was very confident at her interview. She tried not to come across as pushy and cocky but she was after the head receptionist job and hoped that she would be successful.

J.P. was struck by Gabrielle's beauty and confidence and was impressed with her excellent references, so she was shortlisted and in turn was given the job she wanted so much.

In time, with J.P. as general manager, Siobhán as head of catering and Gabrielle heading up reception, the hotel gained a coveted reputation in Ireland and overseas. After two years, it was thriving, having worked out all its initial teething problems, like the air vents in the bedrooms that had not been working for a week at the height of the previous summer. But other than that, there were no major dramas and everything ran smoothly and the hotel soon earned its five-star status.

Gabrielle lived in a flat in Salthill. One day she was off work when J.P. arrived with a bottle of champagne under his arm, along with a bunch of wildflowers to celebrate her birthday. She was pleased to discover that he liked her a lot as a woman, but what she had not realised was that she had developed feelings for him.

She always played it cool where JP was concerned. He seemed to attract women easily, with his charm and good looks. So she had been on guard to ensure that she would not become one of his many casualties, realising that he was also her employer.

But Gabrielle also had many admirers, due to her stunning dark looks and her easy manner, always managing to put people at ease by giving them her undivided attention.

J.P. had noticed many a businessman, various professionals and gentleman farmers who were plainly captivated by this woman's exotic appeal, and when he thought about it, he realised that he felt quite jealous.

J.P. was warmly welcomed into her flat and presented her with the gifts he had brought. Gabrielle was delighted and immediately placed a gentle kiss on J.P.'s lips, much to his surprise and delight. They chatted for almost two hours with J.P.'s eyes fixed on this delightful lady's face, while observing her tiny dainty hands. She was dressed in a beautiful burnt orange body-hugging dress with a red sash wrapped around her slim waist. It felt like a life-changing moment for him and he felt himself falling in love in a way he had never felt before.

J.P. and Gabrielle became more relaxed and they talked about people they had met with a view to future commitments. She admitted that Tim Breslon, a wealthy farmer from just outside Galway, had asked her to marry him a couple of times.

'I have to admit I was very flattered,' she said. 'But he's not for me.'

J.P. began to think in a different way when he heard that, knowing that marriage and her future were being considered by the gorgeous woman sitting opposite him.

'The moment you walked through the hotel door for your interview I had a feeling that my life might change,' said J.P., who had turned down so many attractive women while he lived in London, as indeed Gabrielle had turned down many men when she was in New York.

They drew closer, throwing caution to the wind, and soon they were kissing passionately, both excited at the new life that could await them together. She was thirty-five years old and looked forward to having a husband and children, and hoped her parents back in Jamaica would like J.P., although the Irishman was from a totally different cultural background.

As the champagne had its effect, they both relaxed more and spoke more openly about their feelings. J.P. suddenly asked her the all-important question, to which she replied with a resounding 'Yes'.

Siobhán, Pádraig, Liam and Bridget were excited that J.P. had finally lost his heart to this beautiful woman – and what a major asset they would be to the hotel, making them the dream team when working together.

They had a joint meeting with Father Tom McCabe, J.P.'s Roman Catholic parish priest, and with Reverend Siegfried Coles, Gabrielle's vicar in the local Anglican church, to see how they could incorporate both faiths into their marriage ceremony. J.P. was told that he would need permission from the diocesan bishop for a special dispensation to marry his fiancée because of her different religious background.

Six months to the day J.P. proposed to Gabrielle, they got word from his priest allowing them to be married jointly in his church by the priest and vicar and a date was set. It was agreed that the vicar and priest would each perform separate parts of the wedding ceremony. This was going to be a big affair and lots of preparations needed to be made, involving a large number of people who planned to travel to Galway.

For their honeymoon they decided to spend a romantic week exploring the delights of Vienna.

CHAPTER 56

The wedding approaches

Everybody was very much looking forward to J.P. and Gabrielle's wedding. Jim and Marreese were coming over from London, along with Trudy and Amahil and their young daughter. They planned to travel over a couple of days before the big day, and stay in Siobhán and Pádraig's house.

J.P. asked Amahil if he would stand as his groomsman and if his daughter Adara would be a flower girl. His brother Sean was made best man. Amahil felt honoured to be asked. J.P.'s cousin Jim was also involved, helping people with their seating arrangements.

Amahil asked Trudy why J.P. hadn't asked Jim to be groomsman, instead of him.

'You're J.P.'s best friend, so why wouldn't he ask you?' said his delighted wife. So along with Adara they felt very pleased to share in the lives of this amazing Irish family on such an important occasion.

Uncle Tim was also a very important guest who planned to spend his time at Bridget and Liam's home, as well as enjoying the company of the extended family. They never forgot the major role that Tim had played in getting the children back safely from their evil father in Pakistan. Without him, things could have been very different for everybody.

Sean's wife Hermine was thirty-one and heavily pregnant with their first child – they really hoped that she could hold on until after the wedding! They had clocked up a few years together before they started a family because the farm had taken a lot of time to sort out.

So it was a matter of now or never as they both laughed with J.P., letting him know what was waiting for him and Gabrielle who were in a similar position as they concentrated their efforts on running an increasingly busy hotel.

Orla would be home from Pakistan and had signalled to her mother that she would be bringing someone with her, but she had not yet indicated who that might be.

CHAPTER 57

Living the good life

The intervening years had been very good for gay couple Jim and Marreese, who both loved the London life. They each had an exceptional eye for design, colour and fabric and worked very hard in the highly competitive fashion industry in a city next only to Paris in terms of international fashion prestige. They had also had many lucky breaks and had managed to satisfy a market in fashionable men's outfitting which was always on trend, generating an exceptionally high income for both of them over the years.

They had purchased a building for their business in Knightsbridge, one of London's most expensive areas, and had opened a prestigious boutique in Carnaby Street in Chelsea, which had thrived over the years.

It was all a far cry from their first meeting at a little clothes stall all those years ago. And now, after all their hard work, they were reaping the rewards of their labour.

One of the outward signs of their wealth was their red Jaguar E-Type, and their red setter called Obi, who was never far away.

They created a very comfortable home over their shop, filled with soft furnishings, antique furniture and heavy cream lace curtains in both bedrooms. They had long floral curtains made for their sitting room, and a beautiful large 1930s-style mahogany bed for their bedroom with two singles to match in the spare room.

They could afford to buy a Victorian home in Folkestone, Kent, three years previously and they spent their country weekends there along with Obi, taking Saturday afternoon off and driving back to London on Monday morning, spending a more relaxing life so different to their hell-raising days clubbing in London.

CHAPTER 58

Life after Arslan

Abeer and Ahmed waited patiently for Arslan to come home. Both were anxious, having very low expectations about what kind of a mood he would be in.

Ahmed was devastated to be refused work by his relatives in Ireland. Now he must think of another plan for escaping from this uncaring home and his brute of a father. He did not blame his mother. It was not her fault that he was born with a speech impediment. She too had paid a high price since the day she found out that her second son was never going to be like his older brother. It was then that Abeer knew her life was going to be drastically different from the life she had known before Ahmed was born. Ahmed felt guilty about leaving his mother, but he had little choice if he wanted any kind of a normal life.

Suddenly there was a knock on the door. Abeer ran to answer it, thinking Arslan might have left his keys behind him when he left and suddenly launch into a torrent of abuse against her.

When she opened the door she was surprised to see two uniformed policemen with serious faces standing there. She welcomed them in, wondering what they might have to say.

'Sit down Mrs Hussain,' said one of the policemen gently. He was a tall man with a clipped moustache and a kind look in his eyes.

'Is there anyone else in the house with you now?' he asked.

'Yes my son Ahmed is working up in the garden shed,' she answered, still curious about the reason for this sudden visit from the police.

The other policeman went up to the shed and brought Ahmed back, while the first man sat with Abeer, saying nothing.

'What's the matter?' Abeer asked, feeling alarmed all of a sudden.

Thinking that her life could not get any worse as she shuffled uncomfortably in her chair, Abeer just kept looking intently at the two policemen, totally lost for words.

'Unfortunately, there was a serious accident at North Station this morning,' the first officer told her. 'That is why we are here, to talk to you about what happened there. I'm afraid we have to advise you that your husband, Mr Arslan Hussain, was boarding a crowded train but fell under the train as it left the station and, tragically, was fatally injured. We are so sorry to bring you this awful news. An ambulance took him to Sharif Medical City Hospital.'

'We can take the two of you there now,' said the other man, with genuine sympathy in his voice. 'We need you to formally identify him.'

Abeer and her son were in a state of profound shock, but they readily agreed to go and climbed into the back of the police car that was parked outside.

When all the formalities were done at the hospital, mother and son made their way home.

'This is all like a bad dream,' said Abeer. 'First Abdulla and now your father. What are we going to do? What is to become of us?' she whispered anxiously.

Ahmed took his mother's hand. 'Don't worry Mother,' he said with deep affection. 'I can now take care of both of us. We'll be alright Mother. When all of this is over, we can get on with our lives and never be worried and afraid anymore.'

Abeer had spent most of her life being controlled and slapped around by her angry husband. So what was she to do? Who was she now? She was at a loss, not quite seeing that her life was now her own again. She had not been able to protect her young son from all the years of beatings, being bullied and taunted by his brute of a father. Now all that was suddenly in the past.

For Ahmed, all the years of suffering at the hands of his angry father and even his older brother Abdulla, who had never tried to help him, were finally over. He was free at last – he had no need to be afraid anymore, he was finally out of the shadow of his extremely clever brother, his father's pride and joy. Now he and his jailor father were both gone. Surely all that pointed to a brighter future for him?

Gradually, Ahmed lost his bad stammer, leaving him with only a slight delay in his speech. A more confident man emerged from the shadow of his father. His confidence grew, and he changed his job from making mud bricks to working on building sites, using his skills fully and earning far more money. Life was as good as it got for Ahmed, and for the first time in his life, he had friends and was able to socialise with confidence at the weekends.

Abeer was concerned at the lack of emotion and the absence of support shown towards her by other women. They were all distant now that she was widowed, afraid to have a single woman in their circle who might be a potential threat to their marriages. She nevertheless rebuilt her life and made new friends, joining a women's group that included the Dars, who were good, pious, practising Muslim women. She was happy for the first time in her life, living on a small pension with help from Ahmed. She knew for sure that her dead husband would never walk through her doors again, and that Allah had given their life back, by showing her son and herself such mercy.

Late one Sunday afternoon, Abeer heard a loud knock on the door. Ahmed dropped what he was doing and ran to answer it. He was shocked at who was standing outside. Her features were still the same, even though she had grown into a fine young woman by then. Abeer asked her son who was there, but without waiting for an answer, the visitor made her way through the door. Abeer looked up

– standing there was her long-lost granddaughter Fatima, as she called her, but all grown up and with a young man by her side.

After recovering from the shock of seeing her grandchild after all so many years, Abeer ushered them both into the room. Both granddaughter and grandmother just stood staring at one another for more than a minute before Orla reached out and embraced her and gave her Uncle Ahmed a hug. She introduced Raham as a work colleague, and filled her grandmother and her uncle in on her work with the street children and the poverty-stricken people of Lahore.

Abeer could not believe her good fortune. She was being given a second chance, meeting up with her adult grandchild so unexpectedly. Orla filled them in on her life story, all about her brother and what he was doing at the moment in Ireland. Abeer apologised over and over again for what Abdulla had done to them. Then she told Orla that now there was only the two of them left, as her grandfather had been killed recently in a rail accident.

'They were two very cruel men. Now we have a better life,' said Abeer.

Ahmed nodded his head in agreement with his mother. He was so surprised to see Orla that he had reverted to his former speech problem for a while. Orla listened to him as he tried to speak and walked over to her uncle and put her hand on his shoulder.

'Take your time Ahmed,' she said reassuringly.

After a while, Ahmed was back to his new more assured self and spoke confidently to both of them about his work and his new life, including making friends. Orla had often wondered throughout the years what had become of Ahmed. She was now building bridges, something she thought would never happen.

After two hours, it was time to go. She told both of them that she would call again and made her way back to the safety of the convent, without speaking a word to her friend Raham as she pondered the implications of her visit. She wondered why she felt so insecure, but she felt it in her heart that she had gone back to the house that was full of bad memories for her, all the beatings she had experienced in that very place, and she knew it was time to let go. Raham said goodbye and quietly made his way back to his flat.

Afterwards, Abeer and Ahmed were still in shock at Orla's visit. She would always be Fatima to them. Abeer could not believe all this was happening to her, and how well her granddaughter had turned out. She shuddered with fright, thinking that her granddaughter's story would have been so different if the children had not been rescued. She would have been married off at the tender age of fourteen, a promise her son Abdulla had vowed to keep.

How did she rear such a son as Abdulla? Did she spoil him? Or did he learn his brutality from a young age, seeing how his father treated her and her younger son? His father never raised his hand towards Abdulla, the golden boy, throughout his younger years, but they did raise their fists to each other when Abdulla occasionally stood up to his father, voicing an opinion of his own which his father strongly disagreed with.

Now that they were both gone, she asked Allah for forgiveness, *she'allah, al-hamdu li-llah*. Suddenly she felt happy and fortunate. She felt even more so after meeting her granddaughter after so many years, and hearing the good news about her grandson, delighted that he was going to attend college also, getting a chance of a good education, unlike her son Ahmed.

Life was finally calm for Abeer and her son Ahmed. Their tormentor was gone from their house. Now it was a house they could call a home. It never was a home when all they knew was constant anger. Abeer was at peace with herself at last. She knew she would never let another man cross her door and rob her of her freedom ever again. Ahmed would look after her in her old age, a promise that he made to her on the day they found out that her husband was dead.

Life for Ahmed was good now too. He wrote a long letter to his niece and handed it into the convent where she was staying. He apologised again for not protecting her and her brother and spoke about everything that he thought she might want to know about the family on his side. He told her that in his writing he had no stammer, words fell easily on to the page, and if she wanted to write back to him and wanted to know more, he would fill her in on whatever she needed to ask about.

Abeer and Ahmed never found Abdulla's ashes, but they never wanted them back in the house anyway because they were such a bad memory. When her husband was cremated she asked her son to scatter his father's ashes far away from them both, so they could rebuild their lives in freedom.

CHAPTER 59

One wedding and a baby

Gabrielle's parents and her sister Agap – who was to be her bridesmaid along with Orla – had arrived from Jamaica a couple of days before the wedding and had arranged to stay at J.P.'s hotel. J.P. and Gabrielle had kept rooms on the second floor to accommodate the family.

Orla was due to arrive from Pakistan, and her father Pádraig drove up to Dublin to meet her at the airport, while Siobhán stayed home with Trudy and Amahil and their young daughter Adara.

The excitement was high in the O'Rourke household that day. Liam and Bridget were so excited at how everything had turned out for their children and refused to let their minds drift back to the dreadful earlier years that had plagued the family.

Orla walked through the airport terminal, where her father scooped her up in his arms, giving her a big hug of sheer delight. Raham stood back respectfully and waited to be introduced.

'Raham, meet my dad Pádraig. Dad, meet my friend and colleague Raham from Pakistan. We work together with the poor, the abandoned street children and the disabled in Lahore.'

'So delighted that you were able to come over to our home for the wedding of Orla's Uncle J.P.,' said Pádraig, giving him a warm welcome and a firm handshake.

'They're here! It must be them blowing the horn outside and making that racket,' said a very excited Siobhán.

She opened the door to see the three of them getting out of the car.

Orla made a dash to give her mother the 'hug of all hugs', along with her brothers.

When she saw Amahil, tears immediately sprang to her eyes as she thanked him for saving their lives all those years ago. Trudy and Siobhán stood and looked at this emotional reunion, tears springing into their own eyes in empathy.

Then Orla pulled Raham over and introduced him to the rest of the family.

'This is my friend Raham, everybody,' she announced proudly.

He hoped he looked smart enough for the wedding and was glad that Orla had helped him pick some nice clothes for the occasion. It was very exciting for him to travel so far to Ireland for this special wedding, his first trip outside Pakistan.

Raham really needed no introduction after all the stories the family had heard about the time Orla and Jonathan had spent in Lahore as children. Jonathan remembered Raham with gratitude and thanked him for looking out for the two of them so well all those years before.

Over dinner, Orla and Raham discussed their work with the missionaries, and her basic accommodation in the convent.

'And where do you stay Raham?' asked Pádraig.

He told him he had his own flat in the centre of town. He explained that he just needed his own base and a place for all the files and paperwork associated with his work as a social worker.

After dinner they were ready for bed, but first Orla had to try on her beautiful ruby red bridesmaid's dress and pink satin shoes, just to make sure they fitted well.

'We only have two days left before the wedding,' announced Siobhán in a very excited tone.

Trudy's daughter was going to be a flower girl, and would be wearing a champagne-coloured dress just like Gabrielle's whose gorgeous dress was very like the wedding dress that Princess Grace Kelly wore back in the 1950s.

When Orla got up to her room, Siobhán asked whether her friend Raham was more than just a friend.

'No, not at the moment anyway Mum,' she replied.

The next morning, Orla made her way to the hotel to see J.P. and Gabrielle. It was time for the two women to meet and talk about the wedding. As they were talking, Gabrielle's sister Agap met the family for morning brunch and later the two bridesmaids were fully briefed on their duties for the wedding day.

Back at Orla's home, Siobhán and Pádraig had a leisurely breakfast with Trudy, Amahil and Raham. They spoke again to Raham about his work and about their daughter. He told them how they met all those ago, telling them about how he worked alongside Sister Mary and the nuns in the missionary order. He explained how he got his university education and his job as a social worker, in turn devoting his young life to saving what children he could. His story left his listeners shocked and impressed all at once.

Orla stood in the doorway of her home, wondering if she should bring up her recent visit to her father's house in Pakistan, meeting up with his mother and brother, or whether it would be too painful for her mother to hear.

On the eve of the wedding, Orla decided to talk to her mother about her meeting with her grandmother Abeer and her Uncle Ahmed.

'It has always been unfinished business with me,' said Orla. 'I needed to know more about them and what they thought about their son being killed back in Ireland. I can now finally let my demons go – I walked out of the house one last time and was not afraid anymore.' She also told her mother about the death of her grandfather in a rail accident.

Siobhán listened with interest as her daughter spoke about Abdulla's people. For a moment she was transported back to that dreadful time, what she went through, being so controlled by Abdulla. Now, Siobhán's life with Abdulla was a closed chapter.

Soon it was time for the whole extended family and guests to get dressed and ready for the wedding. All the preparations were complete and it was time to head for St Mary's Catholic Church, Claddagh, which was where the wedding was to take place.

The chapel door was covered with a garland of cream, red and white roses with ivy woven through the roses. The pews were decorated with the same colours, and the altar had four large floral arrangements tastefully spread out.

J.P., Sean and Amahil arrived at the church fifteen minutes early. Sean lit up a cigarette outside the back door of the church to calm his nerves. After one last drag he was ready to take on the responsibilities of the day, including his best man's speech.

Liam, Bridget, Siobhán and Pádraig were sitting up in the top pew. Jonathan and Cathal were in the second pew, along with Trudy and Raham. Hermine and her family sat behind in the third pew. She was feeling a little uncomfortable, sort of hot and clammy, and wished the service was over.

Sean had asked her earlier if she would like to remain back in the hotel but she was having none of it, saying she was looking forward to the big wedding, a day away from the farm and nothing was going to stop her!

Opposite the groom's family were the bride's. Bridget gave them a wave, and everyone settled down to listen to the soft sound of violins.

Adara, the young flower girl, started to walk down the aisle dropping rose petals ahead of the bride and her father, and Gabrielle and her father started their journey down the aisle to the sound of the

Dixie Cups' *Chapel of Love*, a favourite of Gabrielle's. She was followed by her two bridesmaids. Father Tom McCabe and the Reverend Siegfried Coles were the celebrants. Father Tom celebrated the Mass and the Reverend Siegfried gave the couple a special blessing.

After the service and formalities were over, the bride and groom walked, or nearly skipped, down the aisle to the sound of the Beatles song *All You Need Is Love* as all the guests applauded the happy couple.

Hermine just about made it out of the chapel door while J.P. and Gabrielle were signing the register. Severe pains had started the minute she sat down and for a moment she was mad at the baby for coming now, mad at herself for thinking that way and happy all at the same time.

'But Mum,' said Hermine, 'what about Sean? He's the best man – how can he leave his brother's wedding? God, what are we to do? I don't want to steal their thunder but what am I to do?'

'Leave it to me,' said her mother firmly. She said she would call Bridget so she could let Sean know discreetly. But the minute Bridget told Sean, he panicked, and told J.P. that he had to leave immediately.

Amahil was perfectly able to take over as best man, so Sean shoved his speech into his hand. He had no choice but to take Sean's place, and Sean told Amahil that he could add his own bit of banter to the speech as he wished. In his panic he had no intention of waiting for Amahil's reply.

Sean ran down the side of the chapel and out of the door to Hermine, leaving all the guests in a state of shock at his dramatic exit.

'Sorry everyone,' said Hermine, to anybody who could hear.

She thought her labour had started the day before, but she had ignored it. She should have known. She was uncomfortable all night but did not want to cause any upset by speaking to Sean about it.

Sean drove Hermine and her parents as fast as he could to the hospital. Her father got out of the car at one point and tried to sort a very inconvenient traffic jam, but finally a Garda arrived and all was solved in the nick of time.

Bridget and Liam headed to the hospital too, leaving everyone to make their own way to the hotel. J.P. and Gabrielle were excited on both counts – their wedding and Hermine and Sean's impending baby.

'What a great day to be born,' said J.P. to his new wife, kissing her tenderly and hoping that their own baby would follow within a year of married life.

Bridget and Liam followed their anxious son down to the ward. He had appeared from nowhere to tell his parents that they had a new grandson!

Everyone was waiting back at the hotel for news as they drank their Prosecco. All the family made their way back to the hotel for the wedding meal, except Sean of course, though he joined them for an hour later, before his brother and his new wife headed off to Vienna for their honeymoon.

'What name are you calling your baby Sean?' asked J.P.

'We are calling him Milo Sean Liam O'Rourke. What do you think, have we got everyone covered?'

Sean asked his nephew Jonathan and his niece Orla to be the godparents to his first child. Orla felt honoured to be asked and delighted for her brother Jonathan, giving him a bit of responsibility at last.

Milo and Maura, Hermine's parents, were tearful and almost lost for words at the idea of having a little chap to help out on the farm and him being named Milo after his granddad.

CHAPTER 60

A time for reflection

The after-dinner part of J.P. and Gabrielle's wedding was in full swing. It was a time to go with the music and to forget all inhibitions.

Jim and Marreese were having the time of their lives, with Jim pulling his aunty Bridget up to dance and Marreese asking Siobhán to join him.

Trudy, Amahil and Adara were also hopping madly on the dance floor, enjoying the rhythm, along with Gabrielle's sister. Meanwhile, Orla was savouring every moment of this exceptionally memorable bash after a most enjoyable wedding, following her return from Pakistan.

Raham had never seen the like of this before and was enjoying a whole new experience, a long way from home. He thought about how lucky he was to share this wonderful occasion, which was all on account of the chance meeting he had had with Orla and Jonathan all those years ago, when all three of them found themselves in such a desperate situation in Pakistan.

Milo and Maura were celebrating not only this wedding but the birth of a new grandson earlier in the day.

For Siobhán and Pádraig it was a time of reflection as they soaked up the atmosphere and looked around the ballroom. They watched J.P., recognising him as the brother of all brothers. Would anyone else have put their lives on the line as he did for her and her children? Siobhán was so happy for his success in buying and operating such a big hotel so profitably. And now a lovely wife added to his happiness, which she felt was very well deserved.

It was a time to be very thankful for their sons Jonathan and Cathal, who were also plainly enjoying the festivities. They were so proud of how well Jonathan had finally dealt with his troubled past and was applying himself to his study of veterinary medicine at University College Dublin.

Sean too had been lucky, having been touched by the evil hand of Abdulla's cronies in a life-threatening assault and living to tell the tale. It could have been so different, but he survived and was now married to a lovely wife. He was also a father, with a whole new future opening up as a farmer, working a large holding that had huge potential.

And then there were Orla and Raham, in full swing on the dance floor. They thanked God for Orla's life, knowing that things could have turned out so differently. They also thanked God for Raham, still doing heroic work helping vulnerable children who were lost in the dumps, where all those years ago he had met Orla and little Jonathan. Orla was guarded about her feelings for this young Pakistani man, but who knew what the future might bring?

And then Amahil and Trudy of course, part of Siobhán's legacy from her time in London. If not for the deep friendship that had developed between J.P. and Amahil, they might never have got the children safely out of Pakistan. As for Trudy, she was like a sister to Siobhán, and how close they were now, in touch with each other every week.

And of course, Jim and Marreese. They remembered all the kindness they had shown when Siobhán and J.P. first moved over to London, and then later when Siobhán had almost terminated her pregnancy. And they were there for them when they arrived back in London from Pakistan. A dreadful time in her life. And now they are so happy together, having found lasting love.

Finally, there was her old friend Marie and her husband Malcolm. Siobhán thought about how Marie was always there for her – somebody who just listened, never betraying her. Now Pádraig and Malcolm had become friends, cementing their relationship further.

Siobhán and Pádraig looked at each other and were thankful that they had made it as a couple, surviving all the heartbreaks and mistakes of the past. They had no doubt that the hand of God had touched their lives many times, back then and now.

CHAPTER 61

Orla's return and granddad's diagnosis

Raham loved Orla like a sister and was upset that he might not see her again following the announcement of her decision to return to Ireland. But at the same time, he understood that she was at a turning point in her career and needed time to work out where her future life would take her. On an early September morning, she took a long-distance flight from Lahore to London, connecting later with a flight to Dublin.

Siobhán and Pádraig were at the airport to meet her. Knowing that any conversation they would have with her about future plans could be difficult, they resolved to be as sensitive and understanding as was humanly possible.

On the way back to their home in Galway they called in to visit Bridget and Liam for tea.

'It's lovely to be back in your warm and welcoming kitchen again Granny,' said a tired but happy Orla, as she sat down to tea and freshly baked scones.

'It's our pleasure Orla. We are delighted to have you back and hope we see a lot more of you this time,' said her granny as she busied herself around the kitchen.

Orla had always been close to her grandmother and felt she could talk easily to her, knowing that she had a sympathetic ear and an open attitude to life.

Orla knew she would make her decision about returning to Pakistan or remaining in Ireland once she was home and had her feet on Irish soil.

The next morning, Siobhán and Orla called in to J.P.'s hotel, where Orla was looking forward to catching up and seeing their recently arrived baby.

J.P. asked Orla if she would like to help out in the hotel for a while, until she got sorted out. She thanked him for his kind offer, but told him she had already applied for a job in administration in the local health centre and would wait to see if that application was successful. The following week she was called to interview and was awarded a one-year contract, giving her enough time to make up her mind about what to do next.

At the same time, a critical situation was unfolding for her grandfather. Bridget asked Siobhán to accompany her and her father to a medical appointment the following week, as the doctor had specifically asked if someone could come along to support them.

'Thank you for taking time off to come with us love. I have a feeling that we will need you to be with us when we hear what Dr O'Shaughnessy has to say about Liam's condition,' said her worried mother.

All three listened to what the doctor said, but the word 'cancer' went straight over Bridget and Liam's heads.

Siobhán asked if he could explain the diagnosis in more detail, so that her parents could understand things better. The doctor explained that Liam's tests had revealed a definite diagnosis of testicular cancer, adding that there was a range of options available that would give Liam another five or more healthy years.

'But surely Dad can have an operation?' asked a pale and frightened Siobhán.

'Your father's age is against him in this case,' said the doctor. 'Unfortunately, he left it too late to consult me from the time he experienced his first symptoms.'

Liam tried to calm his wife down, telling her he was sure he still had a long life ahead of him, but if it was his time to go, he was ready. This only upset Bridget even more, and tears began to fill her eyes.

'You are going nowhere just yet,' said Dr O'Shaughnessy, 'but we must begin the treatment right away and you must play your part by giving us your full cooperation.'

Later they called on J.P. to break the news. J.P. put his hand firmly on his father's shoulder, telling him that the whole family was there for him as he tried hard to keep any trace of emotion out of his voice. He gave his mother and Siobhán reassuring hugs, telling them that there was no immediate cause for alarm.

Orla was six months into her contract when her grandfather got his diagnosis and began to spend more time with her grandparents. Bridget gently asked her a couple of times when she was going back over to Pakistan and Orla's answer was still uncertain.

'Do you mean you are waiting until after your granddad dies?' asked Bridget in a faltering voice.

'No Granny, of course not. And besides, Granddad is going to be on this earth for a long time yet. There is no need to worry too much, considering the cancer treatments available to patients like him these days.'

Orla went on to confide in her grandmother that she had recently met somebody in the health service who had caught her fancy, and that his name was Seamus O'Suilleabháin.

Bridget was delighted to hear that news and speculated that maybe Orla might not be leaving the country any time soon after all.

CHAPTER 62

Orla's announcement

After a hectic day at the health centre, Orla flopped down on a kitchen chair in her parents' house, where Pádraig handed her a welcome cup of tea.

'I have an announcement to make,' she said with a broad smile on her face. 'I have been dating a lovely colleague called Seamus for some time now. I think you will like him. We have spoken a lot about my work in Pakistan and as he is a qualified social worker himself, we have discussed our future and he has told me he would be interested in going to Pakistan with me. What do you think of that news?'

'We are delighted for you,' said her mother, 'but how well do you know him and are you sure he is fully committed to the big step of going to work with the poor of Lahore? After all, it's a world away from dealing with the social problems of County Galway!'

'I am certain about his level of commitment,' said Orla. 'He is well aware of the challenges he would have to face and I have every confidence in his ability to cope,' she added in a confident voice.

'And what about your idea of possibly joining Sister Mary's order of nuns?' asked her mother.

'During my time back home this time I have given it very serious thought and I have decided that I would be unable to go ahead with that idea. Being with Seamus has opened up a whole new vision in my mind and I think my future lies elsewhere now.'

Orla wrote to Sister Mary after much consideration and told her that she would be going back over to Lahore, but that convent life was not for her. She and her new partner would continue to work with the poor in deprived areas of Pakistan and hoped that she would understand and respect her decision. She also wrote to Raham and told him much the same as she had told Sister Mary, but reassured him that she would be returning to Pakistan and hoped they would have the opportunity to work together again.

Seamus came to tea at Orla's parents' house a couple of weeks later and Siobhán and Pádraig could see how suitable they were for one another, as well as sensing the depth of their commitment to work together in Pakistan.

During the remainder of her contract time with the health centre, Orla and Seamus fell deeply in love, with a proposal of marriage following soon after.

So the girl who had faced more problems in her short life than most was finally coming to terms with her feelings as she looked forward to a long life with Seamus O'Suilleabháin as her adoring husband.

CHAPTER 63

Death in the family

Two years had passed since the wedding of Orla and Seamus in Galway. It had been a lavish affair, on the same scale as the marriage of J.P. and Gabrielle, attended by all their friends from London, as well as Abeer and Ahmed from Pakistan, who made the trip of a lifetime to share Orla's big day.

Orla and Seamus spent two weeks at home in Galway before they left for Pakistan to work with Sister Mary and her group of social workers. They lived in a comfortable flat in the convent grounds and found great fulfilment in their work together.

Raham paid them a visit and told them that he was happier than ever, having started his studies for the priesthood. He was delighted that Orla and Seamus had decided to put some time in with Sister Mary's group of workers before seeking work elsewhere in the vast country of Pakistan.

Bridget got out of the bed one Saturday morning, anticipating a busy day ahead. She and Liam were going over to see Sean and Hermine that day. Hermine was in the eighth month of her second pregnancy with all the excitement that entailed.

She made her way down to the kitchen as usual to cook breakfast for Liam and to make a sponge cake for the afternoon tea at Sean and Hermine's house, where they were looking forward to seeing their little grandson Milo.

She assumed Liam had gone out to feed the animals as he usually did early in the morning, and she was worried when he failed to turn up for breakfast at the normal time.

She called out to him but got no response. She then made her way back upstairs and looked carefully into the bedroom and, to her utter consternation, she saw Liam lying on the floor between the bed and the outer wall, where he had collapsed earlier.

Although he looked as though he was sleeping, Bridget knew instinctively that Liam was dead, but she surprised herself by remaining calm and resigned.

She hurried down the stairs, followed by their dog Patch, and out of the door, walking quickly up the laneway to her neighbour's house.

Betty immediately phoned J.P. at the hotel who in turn rang other members of the family.

Everyone was in total shock. They gathered at Liam and Bridget's house to support her after her grim discovery and waited for the undertakers to come and remove Liam's body. The doctor confirmed that there was no need for a post-mortem as Liam had been living on borrowed time ever since his cancer diagnosis.

Orla and Seamus were informed by phone in Pakistan. She was broken-hearted to hear the sad news and Seamus booked the earliest possible flight home.

Sister Mary told them that the morning Mass would be offered up for her grandfather and her family and asked if there was anything else she might do.

As relatives and friends arrived from far and near for the funeral, tears rolled down Jonathan's face as he was transported back in time. When he was young and very scarred by his cruel life in Pakistan, he recalled the hugely important role his grandfather had played in his life, keeping him safe and focused at a time of chronic insecurity.

For Bridget, it was a time of severe heartache, not only in mourning the death of her beloved husband, but she wondered who was going to keep their farm going. In the days following the funereal, the neighbours kept the farm ticking over, and Milo and Sean lent a hand, dividing their time between the two places until the family decided what to do in the long term.

CHAPTER 64

Life goes on

And so the cycle of life continued for this complex and very varied family, whose lives had spanned Galway, London and Lahore, Pakistan.

Orla and Seamus returned from Pakistan to live and work permanently in Galway. Hermine and Sean and J.P. and his Jamaican wife Gabrielle had second sons, born within days of one another. Liam and Bridget's farm was sold, and Bridget moved into an extension built onto Siobhán and Pádraig's house. Bridget's life was totally changed now and it took her some time to get used to this new life without Liam.

Orla and Seamus were next to expect an arrival and Jonathan graduated in Dublin as a veterinary surgeon, with the family paying for Abeer and Ahmed to travel from Pakistan to Ireland for the second time to celebrate that happy event.

Later, Jonathan announced he was gay and introduced the family to his partner Julian, who was received with joy into the family.

Raham, who had been ordained a Roman Catholic priest, tragically died of malaria while serving in a parish in Uganda, to the deep sadness of Orla and Jonathan.

What had begun with a young man leaving Pakistan, fleeing from his father's anger to seek his fortune in London, and a brother and sister leaving Galway to work in the same city in a spirit of fulfilment and hope for a better future, had resulted in a fatal decision being made by the beautiful but very unfortunate Siobhán O'Rourke.

What took place was not only a cultural clash, but a chain of tragic events that descended into a life of depravity and corruption forced on Siobhán and her two children at the hands of a violent brute whose death finally brought a sense of resolution and happiness, followed by the death of his crazed father – an event which had a similar effect on his wife and younger son.

But with the help, encouragement and love of a close and caring extended family and a strong support system in Ireland, all the suffering and violence and horrible memories experienced in Pakistan and in County Cork were in time gradually erased and those caught up in such chilling events successfully dealt with the demons of their past, including a reconciliation with Pakistani relatives, while moving on to lead lives of great purpose and happiness.

The End

ABOUT THE AUTHOR

Hi there, I am writing under the pen name "A.H. Howard". I have studied the Arts with the Open University and have a diploma in creative writing.

I have worked in public relations for many years.

I live in Ireland with my husband, family and dog Brandy.

Lightning Source UK Ltd.
Milton Keynes UK
UKHW020629021222
413181UK00011B/1634